A Pla

Dr Nigel Barley is [...] Mankind, with special responsibility for North and West Africa. After taking a degree in modern languages at Cambridge, he trained in anthropology at Oxford and gained a doctorate in the anthropology of the Anglo-Saxons. After a period of teaching at University College, London, he was appointed Visitor to the Slade School of Fine Art. In 1978 he embarked on two years' fieldwork in Cameroon before joining the British Museum in 1981. The Cameroon trip was his first experience of anthropological fieldwork – and very nearly his last. But he survived to write *The Innocent Anthropologist* (published in the Penguin Travel Library, 1986). The book is a witty and informative account of his attempts to understand and record the Dowayo society in which he lived. *A Plague of Caterpillars* records Nigel Barley's second trip to the Dowayo people which he embarked on in order to observe their circumcision ceremony, a major tribal event which takes place only every six or seven years.

On the publication of *The Innocent Anthropologist*, the *Daily Telegraph* wrote of Nigel Barley: 'He does for anthropology what Gerald Durrell did for animal-collecting ... a truly remarkable book', and the *Guardian* called *The Innocent Anthropologist* 'one of the wittiest and most unconventional books'. *A Plague of Caterpillars* makes equally inspiring reading.

NIGEL BARLEY

A Plague
of Caterpillars
A RETURN TO
THE AFRICAN BUSH

PENGUIN BOOKS

Penguin Books Ltd, Harmondsworth, Middlesex, England
Viking Penguin Inc., 40 West 23rd Street, New York, New York 10010, U.S.A.
Penguin Books Australia Ltd, Ringwood, Victoria, Australia
Penguin Books Canada Limited, 2801 John Street, Markham, Ontario, Canada L3R 1B4
Penguin Books (N.Z.) Ltd, 182–190 Wairau Road, Auckland 10, New Zealand

First published by Viking 1986
Published in Penguin Books 1987

Made and printed in Great Britain by
Richard Clay Ltd, Bungay, Suffolk
Typeset in Photina

The map on p. 6 is from *The Innocent Anthropologist*
by Nigel Barley (British Museum Publications Ltd, 1983)

Contents

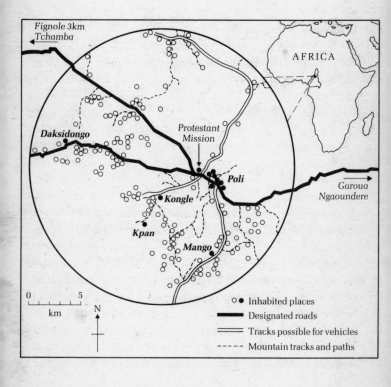

Fignole 3km
Tchamba

AFRICA

Daksidongo

Protestant
Mission

Poli

Kongle

Garoua
Ngaoundere

Kpan

Mango

0   5

km

N

○ ● Inhabited places
━━━ Designated roads
═══ Tracks possible for vehicles
----- Mountain tracks and paths

I

Duala Revisited

'So. You have never been to our country before?' The Cameroonian immigration officer looked at me with suspicious eyes and flicked listlessly through my passport. Stains of perspiration, the shape of Africa, stretched down his shirt under the armpits, for this was Duala at the height of the hot, dry season. Each finger left a brown sweat stain on the pages.

'That's right.' I had learned never to disagree with African officials. It always ended up taking more time and costing more effort than simple passive acquiescence. This was an expedient explained to me by an old French colonial as 'adjusting the facts to fit the bureaucracy'.

In reality, this was not my first visit but my second. Previously I had spent some eighteen months in a mountain village in the north studying a tribe of pagans as their resident anthropologist. Since, however, my passport had been stolen by the enterprising rogues of Rome there was no incriminating evidence in the form of old visas to give me away. I congratulated myself on the bland uninformativeness of my nice new passport. This should all be rather easy. Should I confess to a prior visit, I would immediately be required to engage in an orgy of bureaucracy, giving dates of entry to and departure from the country, number of previous visa and so on. The sheer unreasonableness of requiring a mere traveller to carry all this in his head would serve as no defence.

'Wait here.' I was gestured peremptorily to one side and my passport was taken away to disappear behind a screen. A face appeared over it and scrutinized me. I heard a rustling of pages. I imagined myself being sought in those thick volumes of prohibited persons I had seen at the Cameroonian embassy in London.

The official returned and began a minute inspection of the travel documents of a Libyan of deeply shifty appearance. This gentleman claimed to be a 'general entrepreneur' and possessed an implausible amount of luggage. With breathtaking shamelessness, he had given as the reason for his visit 'the search for commercial possibilities to benefit the Cameroonian people'. To my great surprise, he was waved through without further formality. There followed a whole string of wildly overblown people, a farcical collection of thieves, rogues, art-dealers – all masquerading as tourists. All were accepted at face value. Then there was me.

The official shuffled his papers in a leisurely way. He was taking his time. Having established to his satisfaction his dominance in our relationship, he favoured me with a look heavy with supercilious shrewdness. 'You, *monsieur*, will have to see the chief inspector.'

I was led through a door and down a corridor clearly not for public consumption and given a hard seat in a bare room devoid of all comfort. The lino was scuffed and stained with a thousand sins. It was swelteringly hot.

We are all overdrawn at the moral bank. The slightest challenge by authority draws on deep wells of guilt. In the present case, my position was more than a little shaky. In my first visit to the Dowayos, my mountain tribe, I had learned of the centrality of the circumcision ceremony to their whole culture. But, since it only takes place at six- or seven-year intervals, I had never been able to witness it. True, I had written down descriptions and photographed

8

parts of the ceremony that are reproduced at other festivals, but the real thing had escaped me. Local contacts had tipped me off a month ago that the ceremony was imminent. Who knew when the ceremony would take place again – if ever? It was a unique chance and one to be seized. I knew from previous experience that there was no chance of getting permission in time to do recognized fieldwork; I was therefore entering the country as a simple tourist. For myself, there was no inherent dishonesty in this; I would simply be doing what all tourists did – take photographs. At the ceremony, there would certainly be other tourists, happily snapping away for the scrapbook. It seemed unreasonable that I, as an anthropologist, should not be allowed to do what a vacationing accountant could do.

But now it was clear that they had found out. How? I could not believe that anyone ever read all those pieces of paper I had filled in at the embassy and airport. I comforted myself with the thought that since I was still 1,000 miles away from Dowayoland I could not have committed anything but a trivial offence.

The waiting-room of the chief inspector is not the best of addresses. It would instil despair into those with the most cheery of dispositions. The long delay provided new food for paranoia. I began to fear for my luggage. (A vision of grinning customs men, hands dipping in, dividing up my raiment. 'See. This luggage has not been claimed. We may take it for ourselves.')

At length, I was shown into a spartan office. Seated at the desk was a dapper man with a military moustache and a manner to match. He smoked a long cigarette, the smoke curling up towards a wobbly ceiling-fan set so low as to decapitate any Nordic miscreant who should enter. I was unsure whether to adopt a pose of outraged innocence or French *camaraderie*. Not knowing the evidence against me, I thought 'silly-arse Englishman' would be the best bet. The English are fortunate indeed that most peoples expect them to be a little odd and quite hopeless at documentation.

The dapper official waved my passport, already glaucous with cigarette ash.

'*Monsieur*, it is the problem of South Africa.'

This really took me aback. What had happened? Was I to be expelled in revenge for some English cricket team's fraternizations? Was I being taken for a spy?

'But I have no link with South Africa. I have never even been there. I don't even have relatives there.'

He sighed. 'We do not permit people to enter our country who have been comforting the fascist, racist clique that terrorizes that land, resisting the just aspirations of oppressed peoples.'

'But . . .' He held up a hand.

'Let me finish. To prevent our knowing who has and has not entered that unfortunate country, many regimes are misguided enough to issue their citizens with new passports after they have visited South Africa so that there are no incriminating visas in their documentation. You, monsieur, have just been issued with a brand-new passport though your previous one was still valid. It is clear to me that you have been to South Africa.'

A lizard scuttled across the wall and fixed me accusingly with its beady eye.

'But I haven't.'

'Can you prove it?'

'Of course I can't prove it.'

We pushed back and forth the logical problem of proving a negative until – quite suddenly – the inspector wearied of our rough-hewn philosophy. With true bureaucratic flare, he proposed a compromise. I would verbally declare my readiness to make a written declaration that I had never been to South Africa. This would suffice. The lizard nodded its enthusiastic agreement.

Outside, my luggage lay in a heap, rejected and despised. As I stooped to carry it to the customs desk, my arm was seized by a man of huge girth. 'Psst, *patron*,' he breathed. 'You are going on to the capital tomorrow?' I nodded.

'When you check in your luggage, or when you come back, you ask for me, Jacquo. No weight limit. You just buy me a beer.' He sidled away.

The customs officer was petulant at my long delay with other officials. In pique, he refused to even consider my luggage and gestured me through to where I knew the taxi-drivers lurked.

Somewhere in Africa, there must be taxi-drivers who are kind, peaceable, knowledgeable, honest and courteous. Alas, I have never found this place. The newcomer may expect, with reasonable certainty, to be robbed, cheated and abused. On a previous visit to Duala, before I was acquainted with the geography of the town, I had taken a taxi to a place that was less than half a mile away. The driver had pretended it was a good ten miles distant, charged a huge fare and driven me around in circles until I lost all sense of direction, profiting from my hire to deliver newspapers to outlying districts. Only when I sought to make my way back, did I glimpse the unmistakeable shape of my hotel a mere ten minutes' walk away. Taking an African taxi is almost always hard work. Often, it is much easier to walk.

I took a deep breath and plunged in. Immediately, I was grabbed by two drivers who sought to wrest my luggage from me. In West Africa, luggage is usually treated as a hostage to be ransomed at huge cost.

'This way, *patron*, my taxi waits. Where you go?'

I held on firmly. Scenting an interesting scene, bystanders turned to watch. I was the last passenger for several hours, a prize not to be lightly let slip. An unseemly jostling ensued, myself a bone between two dogs. 'Tell them both to clear off!' shouted a helpful spectator. Knowing this would unite them both against me, I approached a third driver. At once the first two fell to berating him.

Profiting from their distraction, I doggedly made for the door, where lurked a fourth driver.

'Where you go?' I named the hotel.

'All right. I take you.'

'First we agree the price.'

'You give me your luggage. Then we talk.'

'We talk first.'

'I only charge 5,000 francs.'

'The price is 1,200.' He looked crestfallen.

'You have been here before? 3,000.'

'1,300.'

He reeled back in a pantomime of shock. 'Do you want me to starve? Am I not a man? 2,000.'

'1,300. It's already too much.'

'2,000. Less is impossible.' Tears of sincerity started to his eyes. We had clearly reached a plateau where he would stick for some time. I felt strength and determination ebbing away. We settled on 1,800. As usual, it was too much.

The taxi had all necessities, a radio that blared music constantly, a device that simulated whistling canaries when the brakes were applied, a range of amulets that catered for all known forms of faith and despair. The handles that operated the windows had been removed. It seemed to have no clutch and gear changes were accompanied by an ominous grinding noise. Driving was, as usual, a series of wild accelerations and emergency stops.

There is a need in West Africa to test all relationships to destruction, an irresistible urge to see exactly how far one can go. Perhaps I had been inadequately tough in the price negotiations. I saw the driver's eyes home in on a huge woman beckoning to him from the roadside. He slammed on the brakes. There was a short discussion and he sought to embark this vast woman who bore an enormous enamel bowl filled with lettuce. I protested. The enormous lady pushed with bowl and thighs. Cold water slopped down my leg. 'She's going almost the same way. It cost you no more.' He looked hurt. The lady tried to sell me a lettuce. We all argued and shook our fists. The lady threatened to hit me. I threatened to withdraw my custom without payment. We screamed and raged. Finally, the woman withdrew and we drove on totally without rancour or ill-feeling, the driver even humming to himself.

I had arrived some hours ago, cool, relaxed, fattened on six months' convalescence in England. I was already haggard, fatigued, depressed and had not even reached the hotel.

We arrived. The driver turned, a smile on his face.

'2,000.'

'We agreed 1,800.'

'But now you have seen how far it is. 2,000.'

Once more, we went through the rituals of disagreement. Finally, I pulled out 1,800 francs and banged it down on the roof.

'You take this or nothing and I call the police.'

He smiled sweetly and pocketed the money.

Soon I was installed in a small airless room with cool lino on the floor. The air-conditioner gave out a fearful clatter but did produce a gasp of cool air. Fitful sleep came with difficulty.

There came a knock on the door. Outside stood a stout, florid-faced figure in shorts of imperial cut. He introduced himself simply as Humphrey, from the room next door, and spoke in tones of unmistakeable Britishness. He adopted a pose that was not exactly annoyance but more the mien of one deeply wronged.

'It's your air-conditioner,' he explained, 'makes so much noise that I can't sleep at night with it on. The *last* fellow was very reasonable about it and kept it turned off. Very reasonable, he was, especially for a Dutchman.'

'Well, I'm very sorry if it bothers you, but I really can't sleep here with it turned off. The windows don't open. I'd boil to death. Why don't you complain to the manager?'

He gave me a look of withering pity.

'I've tried that of course. Did no good. Pretended he didn't speak English. Come to my room and we'll have a drink and talk about it.'

After several drinks, there developed between us that rank, short-lasting growth of friendship experienced by compatriots abroad. He told me his life story. It seemed he was presently associated with some sort of aid project in the interior, a plan to produce canned fruit juice for export. The project had previously been funded by the Taiwanese but abandoned when Cameroon had recognized Communist China. Humphrey spent most of his time trying to find compatible spare parts for the Taiwanese tractors bequeathed him by the previous administration.

I told Humphrey of my time at the airport. He considered it rather tame. Laboriously, he explained that the man at the check-in desk did not really require a beer but a bribe of a 1,000 francs. I thanked him but I had been here before. Humphrey proposed dinner and led the way to the hotel restaurant. All red PVC and bare bulbs, it recalled something from a Czechoslovak luxury hotel of the 1950s. Lizards slalomed erratically between the light bulbs.

The huge, gleaming, head waiter approached us and pointed at Humphrey's bare knees. 'Go and change!' he shouted. We paused and looked at each other. Humphrey bristled. I could see that he was really angry. Very quietly he said, 'No. I've just come in from the bush. All my kit is being washed. This is all I have.'

The head waiter was unmoved. 'You will go and change or you will have no dinner.' We were both little children before nanny.

Humphrey turned on his heel and stalked from the room with the dignity of a duchess. I was obliged to follow, a pale reflection of his high dudgeon.

In a surge of fraternal solidarity, he confided that he knew of a better place. He looked me up and down appraisingly. 'I don't tell just anyone about this.' I tried to look honoured.

He led the way through the front door to where the taxis waited – and the ladies of the night. Different cultures' views of each other are always interesting. One sure guide is what they try to sell each other. With the confidence with which we expect Americans to want to take tea in a stately home, West Africans assume that all Europeans want to buy carvings and commercial sex. The currently fashionable facial expression in West African cities seems to be one of sultry truculence for ladies. These girls, built like basketball champions, had taken this to their hearts. They shambled around with exaggerated pouts and tosses of their heads. 'Not today, thank you,' said Humphrey firmly.

His taxi-hiring technique was certainly superior to my own. Negotiations were brisk and uncompromising. We embarked. Several of the ladies sought to embark with us. Humphrey repelled them with a paternal hand.

There followed a long drive down dirt roads fringed with jungle. Humphrey gave frequent directions. We crossed and recrossed railway lines that gleamed evilly in the moonlight. Strange odours of rich earth, human excrement and swamp rolled over us. Finally, we emerged on to tarmac near the docks where deserted ships loomed out of greasy water.

We came to a square, formed on three sides by buildings of French imperial style that must have begun to fall apart even before they were completed. Stucco peeled. Creeper had invaded the heavy cement fretwork of the balconies. Confidently, Humphrey led me to the fourth side where jungly plants waged a war against urban firewood collectors, the result being a messy tangle of straggly vines.

'Here we are,' Humphrey breathed heavily.

Memory has a way of playing tricks with us, of intensifying and simplifying. Perhaps I was only seeing it through Humphrey's eyes. But I clearly remember it as the only fresh-painted building in the town. It gleamed in the moonlight. A silver jewel set in a green sea of vegetation. It was a Vietnamese restaurant.

Humphrey was evidently well known here. The hostess, an oriental lady of ceramic beauty, greeted him with a delicate smile and a bow. The proprietor, her husband, was a French expatriate who had spent many years in Indo-China. Honey-coloured children were presented, smiling in a line of descending age, to Humphrey. They bowed and embraced him, referring to him as '*Tonton* Oomfray'. Humphrey became a little maudlin. I thought I saw him wipe away a manly tear. The patron sat with us, pouring cassis and white wine amid mutual reminiscence and discussion of family news. It was revealed that Humphrey had a wife in the north of England as well as what he termed 'a standing arrangement' in the capital.

Over the next hour, we consumed a meal of delicacy and subtlety, flavours and textures exquisitely varied. A tape of gentle oriental music played in the background, a fine-spun filigree of flutes and gongs.

Humphrey waxed confidential over the fruit. 'I feel the need to come here every so often,' he explained. 'I don't come here *too* often or it wouldn't work any more. It gets me away from the sheer gracelessness of Africa. It's the women that are worst – the way they walk, splay-footed and slouching. Look at that!' he cried in awe.

Our hostess glided elegantly over to our table with bowls of lemon-water, setting them down before us in a single flowing movement. With a whisper of fine fabric, she was gone.

It took some coaxing to get Humphrey back to Africa at all. He emerged morose and depressed among the alien vines.

As we entered the square, he suddenly snapped out of it at the sight of a sharply dressed youth of gangling gait over the other side.

'My word. That's precocious.'

This mysterious sentence was clarified when he revealed that Precocious was the nickname of the youth.

'He's a character. Come on.' Humphrey was off.

However clearly Humphrey recognized Precocious, it was clear that Precocious did not know Humphrey. Probably all white men looked the same to him. He bared white, even teeth. 'You want womans?' he inquired with depressing inevitability.

'Certainly not,' said Humphrey.

'Ganja?' He mimed inhalation and a deep ecstasy hardly of this world. He was obviously a man of limited repertoire.

'Cut it out, Precocious. It's me.'

Precocious examined Humphrey somewhat blearily, even raising his fashionable mirror sunglasses. It was evident from his puzzled face that he still had not placed him.

'The white Peugeot.'

'Ah.'

It was clear that Precocious had him now but looked far from pleased. Humphrey, however, insistent upon their good relations, suffered no gainsaying and led us to a neighbouring bar where the story was told – Precocious looking fashionably sultry the while.

Precocious had, in his short life, been much the plaything of Fortune's wheel, with many meteoric rises and dips. At the time of Humphrey's acquaintance with him, he had exulted in the possession of a white Peugeot car that was all his joy. It was not made plain how he had come by the car. This was rather glossed over. It seems that he and Humphrey had gone out to investigate the nightlife at a particularly seedy club called 'The Swamp'. An endearing habit of urban children throughout West Africa is to 'guard' cars for their owners. In fact, it is an embryonic protection racket. In return for a small sum, the car is secure. Should the owner be unwilling to disburse a gratuity, he may well return to find the paintwork scratched, the tyres slashed, the door-locks inoperative.

Seeing Humphrey and Precocious emerge from the car, an innocent child had – in its simplicity – assumed that Humphrey was the owner, Precocious merely his driver. Humphrey had been approached for a 'dash' and refused it. He had been extremely firm in his refusal – some might say too firm.

When Precocious returned to his car, the headlights had been stolen. This, he held to be Humphrey's fault. Humphrey must buy him new headlights. Being both in drink, the discussion had been long and – at the end – heated. Humphrey had been abandoned. Precocious had attempted to drive his car home with, out headlights. There had been a crash. Embarrassing lapses in the documentation of the car had come to light. The car was no more.

Precocious wearied of reminiscence. He turned hopefully to me. I had only just arrived? It was indeed fortunate that I had found him. He was, it appeared, an artist, producing ivory pendants. He displayed some from inside his jacket, making it clear that they were available for immediate purchase. He did not make money by selling them, he emphasized. Indeed he barely covered his costs. For him, they were a means of expressing his artistic soul. They were not normally for sale.

I looked at them. It seemed that his artistic soul had led him to produce miniature ivory elephants, silhouettes of black ladies with complex hairdos – all the normal tourist junk available in every tourist trap the length of the coast. He was forced to sell them, it appeared, to buy new and very expensive drills from Germany with which to continue his art.

Humphrey lent forward. His words dropped like lead.

'He's not going to buy them, Precocious. He's been here before.' He winked at me. 'But maybe he'll buy you a beer.'

Humphrey and I returned to the hotel. The furtive shapes of ladies of the night still patrolled outside. We retired to our rooms. Because Humphrey was now a friend I sweated out a fitful night with the air-conditioner off.

2

To the Hills

Air journeys in Africa always have an unreal quality. One sits, encapsulated, air-conditioned, sipping cooled fruit juice, gliding over the heads of people who stare up from the shade of their mud huts and have never thought to go more than twenty miles from the place they were born. They will live and die within sight of the same mountain. This is not to say that some Africans have not been great travellers. The eighteenth-century journals of writers such as Gustavus Vassa record journeys from Africa to the West Indies, Virginia, the Mediterranean and even the Arctic. But they also bear eloquent witness to the dangers and hardships incurred by anyone so foolish as to venture too far from that tiny area where ties of kinship and blood afford some protection. Most village Africans have a geographical knowledge that rapidly becomes mythical. In my own village no one had ever seen the sea and, at night, old men sitting around the fire would ask me repeatedly whether such a thing really existed. They were horrified at the mere thought of it and, when I described waves, swore they never wished to see such a thing. One seasoned traveller claimed to have seen it at the nearest city some eighty miles away and made much of his description of it. I never had the heart to tell him that he had only seen the river in flood.

We paused at the capital, Yaounde, before flying on to the central plateau where I would try to get a lift back to my mountain people. As the plane taxied to a halt, the stewardess explained to us that we could either stay on the plane or walk over to the terminal for the half-hour we would be on the tarmac.

It is difficult to know which way wisdom lies. What would Humphrey have done? Planes are sometimes flagrantly over-booked, especially during the holidays when schoolteachers sell off the free air tickets they receive on the black market. It is a bold man who lightly relinquishes a seat of which he is in possession. On the other hand, the half hour would doubtless turn out to be a Central African half hour and last considerably longer. A wise man might be availing himself of the limited comforts of the terminal rather than be sitting cooped up in a hot plane. I decided to try for the terminal. This might be the last time I would see a ham sandwich for many months. Alas, I had left it too late. The stewardess shouted at me that I could no longer leave the plane. It was forbidden. I should return to my seat at once.

West African air hostesses are far from the soothing, calming apparitions that haunt cooler zones. Perhaps they undergo the same training as Russian chambermaids and French concierges. They know that their principal duty is to keep passengers in order, to observe and police them. Above all, they are to be obeyed.

On a previous flight, one of my fellow passengers had whiled away such a stop by taking photographs through the open door, possibly accustoming himself to a new camera. It seemed that he was an employee of the company that had built the airliners used on internal flights and wished to proudly display images of his work in action in torrid climes. He was swiftly detected and denounced by a stewardess. There had followed a protracted row with a policeman who accused him of photographing strategic instal-lations and his camera had been confiscated. This flight was more calm. The only distraction was provided by a small girl who was enthusiastically sick in the gangway. The stern stewardess obliged her mother to clear it up.

About an hour later, the other passengers returned with tales of refreshment and delight. There was, of course, no rush for seats. The plane flew on nearly empty, myself chatting to a young American Peace Corps worker on his way to a posting near Ngaoundere.

The Peace Corps is an organization that seeks to promote international understanding and goodwill by sending out its young people all over the world to work closely with locals on various good works. These may range from teaching English to constructing latrines. In Cameroon a number of Vietnam veterans – still in their twenties – devoted themselves to developing the wildlife parks. Large, hairy, gentle giants, they ranged the savannah on motorbikes tracking and counting elephants. The life style of Peace Corps members might reasonably be termed 'informal'. Few return to the United States as clean-cut as when they arrive. Whatever contribution they may or may not make to Third World development, they undergo rapid personal change.

The Peace Corps house in Ngaoundere was always an agreeably ramshackle establishment with all manner of itinerants passing through, to or from the outside world.

The furniture had seen hard use – not many Peace Corps members being of an inclination to flit around with wax polish. Multiple occupancy made it a place of certain dangers. The lemonade bottle in the fridge was as likely to contain photographic fluid as lemonade, the haunch of meat as likely to be part of someone's project on rat-poisoning in the slums as to be for human consumption.

One figure, who lived there for many years, still cast a long shadow. His passage was particularly marked by a strangely raffish animal skin that served as a runner on the scarred and scuffed sideboard. Intrigued by this object, I had asked one afternoon what it was doing in a house otherwise firmly dedicated to the elimination of inessentials. It seemed an odd frippery, like flounces in a monastery.

There was a hush. 'Don't you know about McTavish's cat?' asked an incredulous voice.

It seems that there was a man named McTavish. Having now been firmly ingested by local mythology, he is described as implausibly large and hirsute, of vast appetite and generous sexuality. So great indeed were rumoured to be his inroads into the red-light district that he is declared to have amazed doctors by the richness and strength of venereal infection to which he became host. This proved to be his undoing. He was repatriated and became the object of a medical-research programme. In Ngaoundere, however, his influence lives on. Many a budding friendship has withered on the vine when a young lady would remark to her Peace Corps beau, 'I used to have another friend in the Peace Corps. His name was McTavish.'

Whatever may be the truth or falsehood of this view of McTavish, his presence is clearly enshrined in the cat-skin runner, now a cherished heirloom of the house. McTavish's cat – its name is not recorded in the tale – closely resembled its owner. The result of a cross between a wild tom and a domesticated female, it was large, evil, rapacious and lascivious. Witnesses describe it as having a faint green tinge to its fur though this is not apparent from the runner.

McTavish's cat, the provision of food by its owner having become erratic, took to slaughtering the hens of the neighbours. They attempted to ambush it. It made large detours. They tried to snare it, it smashed their traps and continued to take their chickens. In the end, their protests and claims for compensation could no longer be ignored and McTavish promised to dispose of the cat. Tearfully, he resolved to do it with his own hands. The battle was long and vicious, the cat sneering at poison and avoiding with ease the bolts of McTavish's crossbow. It struck back, tormenting him with its cries at night. Finally, one sultry afternoon, McTavish cornered it behind the water tank. It knew its last hour had come but resolved to sell its life dear. The struggle was terrible but there could be only one outcome. The cat perished and McTavish retired to lick his wounds. The battle had, however, been observed by an employee of the electricity company. Seeing the cat was dead, he asked McTavish to allow him to eat its eyes, having been told that this would give him second sight. McTavish, never a man to turn down a new experience, allowed this. One thing led to another and a fit of utilitarianism seized McTavish. Good meat was scarce. He curried the cat and tanned the hide. It is not clear whether those who dined there that night were told what they were eating before they did so. So great was their rage at this culinary incest, however, that several were taken ill and friendships ruptured beyond repair. The remains of the curry lurked balefully in the fridge for a month, then were flung outside. Neighbours reported that they were eaten by a wild cat. Its fur had a green tinge.

The young American was not downcast at the tale of McTavish's cat, being creditably full of youthful enthusiasm and high ideals. He revealed that he had come to help construct fish ponds on the plateau so that the protein content of the local diet could be improved. I remembered the case of another Peace Corps man who had previously worked on this project and concluded after several years that his principal achievement had been to increase the incidence of water-borne disease by some 500 per cent.

Even on fieldwork, there are short intervals when not everything goes wrong. We arrived at Ngaoundere, said our farewells and I was able to gain the Protestant mission station without incident but with my luggage.

It is a mark of the seasoned traveller that he knows what to turn up with. In Cameroon, one does not bring a bottle of wine but a Christmas pudding and a large tinned Cheddar cheese. These assure instant welcome.

To my considerable surprise, my letter had got through to Jon and Jeannie Berg, my local missionaries in Dowayoland, and they had delayed their departure from the city of Ngaoundere to wait for me. We could leave for the mountains the next day.

The drive was long and followed the usual pattern. As we got to the edge of the escarpment that divides the central plateau from the northern plain, there was the usual torrential rain and thunderstorms. As we descended the precipice, whining in bottom gear, the heat rose to a stifling 100 degrees and there followed the long drive along patched tarmac to the dirt road to Poli.

As soon as we reached this point, it became clear that there had been changes. On my first trip, the road had been so full of rocks and craters that I had seriously wondered at several points whether I had turned off it in error. Now, the influence of the new *sous-préfet*, the representative of the central government, had made itself felt. The road was astonishing, smooth and broad as a new runway, a bright-red ribbon that cut straight through the bush. True, by the end of the rainy season it would again be rutted and eroded, but it was a shocking sign of optimism and endeavour in a town that had long reconciled itself to neglect and decay.

At the end of the long haul down into Poli, there were other changes. In the market, scales were being used to weigh the produce instead of the rather impressionistic measures that had hitherto prevailed. Prices were clearly displayed. There was – incredibly – meat on sale. True, all this seemed to have served to depress the traders rather than raise their spirits but there was an unaccustomed bustle about the place.

We pulled up at the mission station to a rapturous welcome from

Barney, the Bergs' Alsatian dog, and a hardly less ecstatic greeting from Ruben the handyman.

We went into a long routine of, 'Is the sky clear for you?' 'The sky is clear for me. Is it clear for you?' and more in like vein, the normal greeting formulae. But Ruben's heart was not in it, his eyes kept sliding to the rear of the truck where lay a brand new Nigerian bicycle, still in its wrappings.

Like most West Africans, Ruben was crippled by chronic debt. This was not simply the result of shortage of cash in the face of consumer desirables. It is rather a traditional way of life. While Westerners groan beneath the burden of buying a house, Africans mortgage themselves up to the hilt to buy a wife. West African magazines are full of the misery caused to young men by the need to stump up large amounts of money and cattle before they can wed. Youth rails against the system but no one is willing to be the first to give his daughter or sister away for nothing. If he did so, how would he, in his turn, be able to buy a wife for himself or his son? And so it continues. Dowayos were always incredulous when I told them that 'in my village' we gave our daughters away for nothing. One Dowayo of entrepreneurial flair but low ethnographic awareness asked if I could not have a consignment shipped over. We could marry them off and keep the bride-price for ourselves. It all seemed eminently sensible.

As a result of marriage payments, Dowayoland is in a constant state of litigation. Payments are spread over many years and all a man's kin will be expected to help. Almost inevitably, at some time a man's wife will run away even if only to frighten him into submission on some matter of domestic strife. He will try to get back the bride-price already paid. His wife's kin will try to get him to complete payments. His own kin will ask politely what has become of their contribution, until he sees no way out. Unsettled debts will be remembered for several generations and inherited.

Dowayos intrigue endlessly over these old scores. Like chess players, they have the ability to plan several moves in advance. The ultimate coup is to collect on a debt that was thought unenforceable. Thus, if A owes a cow to B who owes one to A's friend C, A may well give the cow to C and allow him to collect on an old debt that everyone else would have given up as a lost cause. B should have foreseen the danger of course and disposed his debts with greater skill.

It is impossible to live long in such a climate of raging debt without getting sucked into the system. I ended up in the debt of the mission. The chief was in debt to me but my assistant owed his wife money which she had lent to the rain-chief. All this made buying or selling anything fraught with difficulties as the money of the transaction was likely to disappear somewhere along the chain in liquidation of some quite different debt, incurred perhaps years before.

Ruben's own finances were as complex as those of a Swiss multinational corporation but yet he pined desperately for a bicycle. There was no way in which he could ever hope to save up enough to buy one as everyone knew exactly how much he earned and had allocated it in advance. So Ruben had come to a secret accord that instead of being given a rise in recognition of good service, he should be 'given' a bicycle and his rise be withheld until it was paid for. This, of course, constituted a considerable interest-free loan but it also opened up whole new areas of debt and obligation that had not been foreseen – at least not by anyone but Ruben.

The chief quality of this particular model of bicycle, apart from its enormous weight, was the incorporation of a special sort of bolt. These were made of a curious alloy, possibly devised specially for this purpose. Be that as it may, they had the infuriating habit of simply twisting apart when anyone attempted to remove or tighten them. The result was a heavy trade in spares with the city some hundred miles away. Myself, the missionaries, the doctor and schoolteachers, in fact anyone who travelled, would be expected to act as a buying agency for spares. The model had been much altered over the years, the size of the bolts had changed, one could never be sure that any part would fit. Naturally the intermediary was held responsible for any inadequacies of parts provided.

Whenever Ruben's machine demonstrated temperament, he looked sad, sighed greatly and dramatically all over the house, generally transforming the atmosphere into that of a funeral parlour. Finally, it could be borne no longer and new parts would be supplied on credit at which he would smile dazzlingly and fill the house with song. Somehow, he always managed to create a lingering feeling of guilt that he had been supplied with such an inadequate machine.

It was only a matter of weeks before a Dowayo came to me in the village asking for a loan because Ruben had a way of getting spares but insisted on cash on the nail. I never inquired too closely into it, but I suspect that, for a consideration, parts could be exchanged between the clients' and Ruben's bicycle. The defective part was then displayed by Ruben as evidence of the unworthiness of the machine Jon had purchased. A replacement would then be rapidly supplied on credit by Jon, while Ruben enjoyed immediate payment and charged for the service. He had converted his bicycle into a bank.

But Jon's own concerns were far from Ruben's financial speculations. Undeterred by my own catastrophic attempts to coax the local soil to bear fruit, he had constructed a garden on the hill beneath his house. A system of barricades and entanglements had been erected to keep out marauding cattle whose tendency to 'ravage' was proverbial. There sprouted melons, beans, peas, all manner of exotic plants beneath the passing gaze of wayfarers. Each paused to give his word of advice. Most predicted doom after the fashion of farmers the world over. But Jon soldiered on and the watering of the crops was an evening ritual that brought him deep satisfaction as well as blisters. As I had before him, he doubtless feasted in his mind on huge sweet peas and succulent squashes, and slavered as he laboured.

The sun sets swiftly in the tropics, giving way to deep darkness with a short period of twilight. A gibbous moon rose with indecent speed over the jagged granite peaks. Away in the hills, bright-red dots marked the place of bush-fires burning away the rank grasses so that fresh growth would follow. The heat, the susurration of a million crickets, the gentle moonlight, all made the verandah a good place to doze off. From the garden came the sound of Jon chortling gently over his swelling melons, from the backyard, the delighted chuckles of Ruben as he stroked the glossy black paint of his gleaming new bicycle, the first totally new thing he had ever possessed. In the kitchen, Marcel, the cook, wrestled despairingly in French with an English Christmas pudding and prayed for rain. It all seemed totally normal.

3

Rendering unto Caesar . . .

Arrival in a West African town involves a European in a number of 'formalities' that are neglected at his peril. They imply a curious mixture of self-importance and self-abasement. The average visitor will be amazed that the authorities should care one way or the other about his presence in their fair town. But should he fail to comply with the regulations, he is liable to be 'discovered' as a spy or worse. So there is a fairly depressing circuit whereby one's presence is announced, rather as in earlier days Europeans would leave their visiting cards at strategic locations.

Inevitably, the first visit was to the chief of police, armed with all relevant documents.

As I set off down the road to town, I met many familiar faces, some Dowayo, some townsmen of Fulani or southern extraction. Politely, they inquired after the well-being of my wives and my millet crop. I did the same to them.

It had come as a great surprise to me when I visited Africa for the first time that I was unable to recognize individual Africans, being overwhelmed by superficial differences. It is rather like one's experience before a gallery of paintings of gentlemen in periwigs. Once one has got to the third, the others have disappeared from the memory. I was pleased now to be able to remember the names of the people, whom I had not seen for some time, until I came to one man who clearly knew me well but was a total blank in my recollection. With embarrassment, I realized that the problem was that he had changed his shirt. Most Dowayos only possess one shirt for everyday wear, so inevitably, they wear the same one all the time. Although they normally wash themselves on the way home from the fields, they almost never wash their clothes, simply wearing them to the point of disintegration and sometimes beyond. The beginner learns to recognize people by their clothes rather than their features.

At the police post, there were two or three cheerful young men in baggy khaki uniforms, lounging around, having removed their boots to ease their feet. They were pointing out the various scars and wounds on their toes and heels, each one recalling a past injury or adventure.

'This is where I was bitten by a snake. All were amazed that I lived.'

'Here is where I fell from my motorbike during training. The pain was very great.'

Africa is hard on feet.

A solitary prisoner was humming to himself as he painted the white stones that edged the flagpole. Above, the flag hung limply in the still air.

I was greeted by one of the recruits I knew from my last visit, an earnest Christian who was doing a correspondence course in French language. 'Welcome. You have returned. What is the French word for someone who owns a grinding mill?' He chewed on a pencil and looked worried.

A corporal appeared from inside, distinctly less jovial than the loungers. His first move was to warn me that I was on government property and must take no photographs. Since I had no camera with me, this was a redundant instruction, but one accepted with due meekness. We proceeded to an inspection of my passport, with much suspicious scowling and holding up of stamps to the light. It was regrettable that the chief had departed on a mission of importance and delicacy to Garoua. Only he could take the step of allowing me to sign my name in the large book kept for aliens. How long would he be? Should I wait? This was not foreseeable but they would call the police headquarters in Garoua to verify whether he had left yet. A large radio was produced from inside the cupboard and the corporal began shouting into it amid bursts of hiss and static. A faint voice, as of a drowning man, could be heard saying something with great insistence, then in a brief pause could be heard to ask very clearly 'What do you want?' to which the corporal replied 'Who?' before the static closed in again like fog.

'Adverse meteorological conditions,' announced the corporal with finality, folding down the aerial. We both looked at the perfect blue skies over the mountains. It seemed unpolitic to say more, so I prepared to take my leave.

At that moment, a somewhat raddled Land-Rover drew up in a cloud of dust. Its green canvas top had been replaced by one of sky-blue and domestic manufacture, giving it a holiday-camp air. From this, disembarked the chief, a trifle hot and dusty but with the air of a man having come from a job well done.

'I can't possibly talk to you now,' he declared. 'I've been to get urgent supplies. Come back tomorrow at eleven.'

As I moved off, I peered in the back of the machine. As I had guessed, it was full of beer. Subsequent investigation revealed a rumour that the vehicle was used to haul beer down to the villages on the River Faro, some thirty miles away, otherwise devoid of drink. There, it was claimed, it sold for fabulous prices.

If this was so, then it was one of the police chief's more benevolent functions and he doubtless deserved the small profit so riskily gained.

At the other end of town, the dank and depressing sous-préfet's

32

office that I recalled. had been spruced up by the application of a coat of whitewash. White-robed, clerkly figures shuffled in sandals from room to room with handfuls of papers. Admittedly their gait was hardly swift but it was the first time that anyone had been seen moving about at all in that building. The clerk who controlled admission told me that the *sous-préfet* was not available. Being a Dowayo, however, he revealed that he might be found if I dropped in on the town chief.

In many parts of Cameroon, when the colonial forces arrived, they found a system whereby Fulani overlords ruled over pagan peoples. They found it convenient to generalize this system to parts where Fulani incursors had not reached, as at Poli. There is now a Fulani chief in the town who sits on the native court and claims jurisdiction over the area. Local Dowayos resent this very much and have as little to do with him as possible. As far as they are concerned, *they* were never defeated by the Fulanis. He would certainly not be welcome in their villages.

On my previous visit, he had not exactly endeared himself to me. As the proprietor of the mail truck, he had a virtual monopoly of transport between Poli and the big cities. Being very close to the old *sous-préfet*, he had worked hard to ensure that no bus service was permitted, no petrol sold, no one else allowed to carry passengers. Because the presence of a foreigner would attract the attention of the police to his always illegally overloaded truck, he had always made it as difficult as possible for me to travel on his vehicle, going to such lengths as changing the pick-up points or days of departure when I was out of town. A further source of friction had been his determined attempts to make me take out membership in the one political party permitted in Cameroon – an operation on which he received a commission.

However, time having blunted our antipathy, I resolved to seek out the *sous-préfet* in his lair. I had the awful fear that somewhere in the hills the rite of circumcision was even now being carried out as I wasted time in town.

After much hand-clapping outside the chief's house, a small boy appeared and scuttled off to announce my arrival. In due course, I was shown into a small round hut with a floor of gravel. The walls were painted with geometric Fulani motifs and the overall effect was of a clean and pleasant dwelling. Stretched out on rugs on the floor were the chief and the *sous-préfet*. They were listening to Arab music on the radio. As I entered, the chief tucked a bottle of whisky deftly into his robes. It looked like a movement refined by many years' practice.

The *sous-préfet* rose and greeted me. He grinned and addressed a few words in Fulani to the town chief who scowled, drew forth the bottle and poured me a small quantity in a glass stamped 'Souvenir from Cannes'. We settled ourselves and the *sous-préfet* began to discourse in perfect French on his plans for the town. His eyes gleamed enthusiastically behind his glasses as he told of piped water and the re-installation of mains electricity (a convenience that had been allowed to lapse since the departure of the French). He was determined to have a telephone before two years had passed. 'My job is to animate,' he explained. 'I have already explained to my friend here', he indicated the chief, 'that his house may have to be demolished for my telephone exchange.' He giggled wickedly to which the chief returned a wan half-smile.

'I am determined to make the Dowayos active. You will please supply relevant information.'

The ethics of anthropology are not easy. The anthropologist normally attempts to influence the people he is studying as little as possible but knows that he must have some effect. At the best, he may restore to a demoralized, marginal people something of a sense of their own worth and the value of their own culture. But, by the very act of writing the standard monograph on any people, he

34

presents them with an image of themselves that must be coloured by his own prejudices and preconceptions since there is no objective reality about an alien people. The use they make of this image is unpredictable. They may reject it and react against it. They may also change to conform more closely to it and become ossified actors portraying themselves. Either way, innocence, the sense that something is done because this is the *only* way things can be, is lost.

During the colonial era, anthropologists always had a very uneasy relationship with the authorities, who wanted to use them to change people. Now, it seemed, it was happening to me. 'Why are the Dowayos so lazy?' he asked.

'Why are you so energetic?' I retorted. He laughed.

He waved at me a copy of a book by Mrs Gandhi. 'I have been reading this book by the daughter of Gandhi. She says many good things about the evils of colonialism.'

I told him that Mrs Gandhi was not Gandhi's true daughter. He looked shocked. 'But how is this possible? This is dishonest. Are you sure?'

Thereafter, he questioned me on almost every occasion we met, whether or not Mrs Gandhi was indeed the true daughter of Gandhi. I began to wonder myself, my former certainty sapped by his anxious inquiries. It seemed that the matter was crucial to the value of her book. When I returned to England and was met by friends at the airport, they must have thought it odd that the first thing I asked them was: 'You know Mrs Gandhi? Well, is she the true daughter . . . ?'

I mentioned to the *sous-préfet* that I had just been to see the police chief and wondered whether he knew of the surreptitious beer business in which he was engaged. He giggled. 'There was a time when he made you sweat a little.'

He was referring to a time when I had got lost in the bush at night and, heading for the nearest light, had ended up behind the house of his assistant. The police chief had immediately been firmly convinced that I was spying and given me an anxious moment or two as he interrogated me.

'He is a good man,' said the *sous-préfet*, 'perhaps a little over-zealous at times.' He grinned, leaning forward, and prodded me with the collected wisdom of Mrs Gandhi, 'I kept my eye on him, you know. I wouldn't have let anything happen to you.'

I thanked him profusely and withdrew, liking him even more than before, glad that he had confounded all those who had been convinced that the dogged stubbornness of Poli and its inhabitants would swiftly break his optimism. The town chief had not said a word and only grudgingly shook hands when I left.

In the street, the first rains had begun to fall, big wet drops running along the surface of the dirt as if over hot iron. I trudged on in the thick dry-season dust, the street suddenly full of little boys who screamed and swooped with joy, holding out their robes for the sheer pleasure of being wet and cool.

By the time I had reached the bridge to the mission, the river had become a raging torrent and there was no possibility of crossing. Such was the force of the water that your legs would simply have been washed out from under you. Besides, I was not eager to plunge my pristine feet, laboriously debugged in England ('See, this is where I had riverworm. Here they removed jiggers.'), into this, the first flood of the year. Notoriously, this was the spate that washed downstream a whole year's accumulated filth and pollution.

When I finally arrived at the mission, darkness was falling. The only dry clothes I could find were long Fulani robes that Jon and Jeannie had bought as a souvenir. Marcel and Ruben went into hysterics as soon as they saw me and mercilessly followed me around calling out '*Lamido, lamido*' ('Chief, chief').

4

Once More unto the Breach

Having covered my back with the authorities, all that was needed
to become a going concern again was to regain control of Matthieu,
my erstwhile assistant. I knew from letters I had received in
England, long rambling disquisitions in which problems of bride-
price played a large role, that he was seeking to enter the customs
service. This, he had confided, was an assured means of enrichment
but he feared greatly being posted to a remote border area away
from other members of his tribe amongst 'savage bushmen', who
would have appalling customs and eat vile food. Were there even
Christians in the far north of the country? He was unsure.

Inquiries among the gilded youth of Dowayoland, the strollers
up and down the town's one street, the loungers at the Adamoua
bar, revealed that he had waited many months for the result of his
entrance examination and then given way to the sin of despair and
returned to his village. I determined to seek him out.

Once again, the mission came to my aid, sparing a long trek out
towards the river in the hope of a lift on a passing truck. I was
equipped with a fine van, hired at cost, and vowed to set off at dawn
the next day, pleasurably anticipating the empty solitude of the
bush.

There is, however, a strange intelligence service that observes
such enterprises. As I emerged from the house the next day in the

first cold light of dawn, there stood a group of people, luggage heaped at their feet, who knew precisely where I was headed and were resolved to accompany me there, if not further. One rapidly comes to accept the presence of such a band of companions as inevitable. It would have been an almost uncanny experience – a sudden hush in a crowded room – had they not materialized. Refusal was, of course, impossible. We embarked without formality in a furious jostling and shouting. It required great firmness to establish that I must have sufficient space to reach gear-lever and brakes, this space being only grudgingly granted. I announced formally where I was bound. They nodded agreement. Of course. This was understood. Let us leave at once. Bundles of yams, clothes and furious chickens, their feet tied together to make a carrying handle, were adjusted and we set off. The journey was uneventful. There was only one fight caused by the chickens of one woman pecking the child of another. One passenger sought to stop us as we headed for the country so that he could drag forth from concealment a wife and six large bundles of indeterminate material. This ploy was denounced with rage by all the others and so the man abandoned his wife and continued with us alone. Peanuts were passed around and enjoyed with much lip-smacking and joking about their purgative effect on women.

Suddenly, I saw a sight that made me slam on the brakes and shout with excitement. There, disappearing at speed into the scrub, was a bizarre, bulky figure. At first sight, it was approximately conical and about six feet tall. A tall cone of wickerwork, covered with leaves and creeper, possessed of two arms and feet, it swayed perilously as it rushed into the bush. I knew from descriptions that this was no mirage, monster or friendly English Green Man. It was a boy, circumcised some months previously, and moving around shielded from the gaze of women by this head-to-foot covering.

I pointed to the rustling mass. 'When was that boy cut?' Immediately, there was an explosion of shocked titters, denials that there had been anything in the bush at all. The women averted their eyes or covered their faces with their hands. The jostled chickens screeched. A child wailed. I knew well that – infuriatingly – these matters could not be discussed in front of women but it took great self-control to choke back frustrated questions. This, after all, was why I had come all this way. Did it mean that I had missed the ritual by several months, that it was already finished?

We drove on, myself plunged in gloom until the turn off that led to Matthieu's village. Was not this the path? I inquired. There came a silent chorus of shaken heads. Surely the man the *patron* sought was several miles further on? It would be wise anyway to continue to the Catholic mission that was only another five miles. There, proper inquiries could be made. All these bush villages looked the same. It was not to be expected that I would be able to tell one from another. A chorus of nods.

Unfortunately for my passengers, this was the moment that Matthieu's mother chose to emerge from the tall grass. As we spoke, magically they melted away. Yes, her son was at home. She would take me to the fields.

Matthieu was crouched over his hoe, blade slashing away at the roots of a recalcitrant weed, like some heavily symbolic tableau representing African toil. Gone was the green glossy suit. Sweat coursed down his face – considerably thinner than when he had been in my employ – and in his throat rumbled a hoeing song. Dowayos accompany most rhythmic activities with song, turning dull, repetitive work into a sort of dance. His father, a wizened old man of piratical aspect, spotted me first, tapped Matthieu on the shoulder and pointed towards me. Matthieu dropped his hoe and ran – arms outstretched – across the field as if in parody of the opening scene of 'The Sound of Music'.

'You have come back?'

'I have come back.'

'You are working?'

'I am working. I am here for three months only. Will you come with me?'

'I will come.'

Like rising sons the world over, Matthieu interrupted all my attempts to talk to his father. 'I will tell him I am leaving. It is of no importance.'

We retired to Matthieu's new hut. When the Dowayos had built me a new hut, they had insisted that it should not be round – like their own habitations – but square like the school, police post and prison. For a White Man to live in a round hut would be most improper.

Matthieu had built himself a dwelling that was a replica of my own, a square hut only slightly larger than traditional huts but a clear sign that association with me had to some extent removed him from his own culture.

We talked of the news. As ever, Matthieu's world centred on the price of women. His plans to marry a twelve-year-old girl had fallen through because her family had been too demanding. Knowing that Matthieu had worked for me, they had immediately assumed that he must be rich. He looked sorrowfully at me as if in reproach. I groaned inwardly, knowing that the request for a contribution to the bride-price could not be long coming, that I would be unable to provide the huge sum demanded but would end up paying something, leaving me feeling both impoverished and guilty. Finally, we got around to the subject of circumcision. It was always a touchy subject with Matthieu. Being a modern-minded Christian, he had had the operation performed with an anaesthetic at the hospital instead of suffering the rigours of traditional genital mutilation. For this, he would be mocked all his life by other Dowayos who would accuse him of cowardice. He would, moreover, be isolated in many crises of life, not possessing a group of 'brothers of circumcision' who had been cut with him and would perform for him the most important ritual duties.

He denied all knowledge of what was afoot in the mountain villages but would make inquiries and rejoin me in three days' time. In the meantime, perhaps I could give him an advance on his salary . . . ?

Back at the road, another group of Dowayos headed for town had mysteriously assembled, including Gaston, from the village where I had lived, his bicycle magnificently garlanded with wrapping paper and plastic flowers. Was this a new bicycle? He looked embarrassed. No, *patron*. But there was someone at the mission who did have a new bicycle and he had sold the wrapping paper to Gaston to embellish his own machine so that people would think that that was new too.

We embarked the passengers, the bicycle, the yams and the chickens, but I set my face firmly against a goat. The owner departed in a huff.

Gaston spoke French so we were able to speak about circumcision – none of the women understanding the language. Stealing furtive glances around us and conversing in whispers, we discussed the boy I had seen earlier. It seemed there was no need for me to worry. He was not Dowayo. He was Pape from a neighbouring tribe with similar customs. They circumcised at a slightly different time. It was a mystery why he should be so far to the east. Surely no one would feed him round here. It was outrageous that he should wander around here, endangering the fertility of Dowayo women, not that of Pape maids. If he were caught, the men would beat him. Gaston blushed with anger.

Gaston had heard that the ceremony was indeed to be held over by the rain-chief's mountain but did not know when. He would inquire. A cousin of his was a circumciser and would surely attend any such event, since many boys would be involved. I dropped him off, together with the embellished bicycle, at the turn-off to Kongle, asking him to tell Zuuldibo, the chief, that I would visit him the next day.

A present would be necessary. I would need some beer.

At the bar in Poli, the schoolteachers had already settled in for the day. As usual, they were involved in financial wrangling. This time, however, it was not the totally unpredictable deductions made by the tax authorities from their salaries that were at issue, but the proper bribe to pay for importing a motorbike illegally from Nigeria. I lent an ear. This might be of interest to Matthieu.

There were rumours all over town about a consignment that had come in. Apparently, someone had happened upon a broken-down truck over the other side of the Faro, loaded down with tyres and motorbikes. He had been lucky to escape with his life having been pursued by the smugglers. The next day when he had nervously crept back along the same stretch, there was no sign of the truck. Even the tyre tracks had been effaced. But the consignment had arrived – no one knew how – in Poli. The police were inquiring into which trucks had been out towards the river recently. They looked significantly at me and at the truck I was driving.

A man, a Pape farmer judging by appearances, shuffled in and bought a beer. He looked at me knowingly rather after the manner in which drunken Glaswegians are wont to eye those they are about to hit and approached me making writing notions. In surprisingly good French, he asked politely if I could lend him a pen and paper. The pedagogic urge is a long time dying even in one who has worked in universities. Ballpoint pens are very hard to come by in Dowayoland. They cannot even be bought in town. One is obliged to go some sixty-odd miles to get one. A sure way to cause a near riot is to drop a pen anywhere near a school for it will be pounced on by a hundred eager children. I was, therefore, happy to help the man out. He settled himself at a table and wrote out a long letter with painful slowness, carving each character into the page between great bouts of pen-sucking and rolling of eyes towards the ceiling. The schoolmasters sniggered at the clumsiness of his horny fingers. Meanwhile, I opened negotiations for some beer to take to Zuuldibo.

The great problem is bottles. There is a great shortage of bottles, many being abstracted from the system and diverted to purposes quite foreign to those for which they were designed. Dowayos convert them into musical instruments, lamps and hide-scrapers. They use them to contain honey, water and herbal remedies, amongst other things. There is a vigorous trade in empty bottles. The result is that beer-sellers are reluctant to let fresh bottles out of their grasp unless they receive an equivalent number of empty ones. This doubtless has the worthy effect of preventing a man going to the bad by doubling his beer intake overnight. It works quite well once you have the empty bottles to trade with. Acquiring the first empty bottles is, however, the flaw in the system. It is virtually impossible. I am tempted to recommend that bodies conducting research in former French West Africa should keep a central supply and issue two to each fieldworker. It would enormously improve the efficiency of their workers. This time I was lucky in that I had borrowed two bottles from Jon. My misfortune was that they were not of exactly the same type as those I wished to carry away with me.

Like many other such problems it was treated rather as a series of hats to be tried on in a mirror, a source of diverting theoretical stances to be slowly savoured, rather than as an impediment to progress to be resolved as quickly as possible. The schoolteachers joined in. Some berated the barman for his unwillingness to part with the bottles. Others applauded his determination to refer the whole matter to the owner who would surely return before nightfall. The Pape farmer laboured on. Finally, one of the teachers tired of this intellectual flirtation. He would sell me two of his own empty bottles. This bold lateral move was applauded like the winning gambit of a chess-master. It had taken half an hour and cost me half as much again as anyone else, but I managed to buy and carry away two bottles! I prepared to bear them off in triumph.

As I was about to leave, the somnolent scribe seized me and pushed into my hand the screed he had so painfully composed, together with the pen I had lent him. I read it with difficulty.

The letter was written in French, couched in terms appropriate to a high-level ambassadorial exchange of the seventeenth century. It began with the florid phrase, 'I address myself, dear Sir, to your high benevolence.' In short, which it was not, it was a request for a loan. It appeared that 'my brother', the French missionary, had departed for the city and tarried there a day longer than expected. This man, his gardener, had therefore not been paid on time and I should immediately make good his loss, or as the letter put it, 'disburse non-receipted money'.

The ethnography of communication is a matter of some interest to anthropologists for every culture has rules about what may and may not be said and a way of matching styles to content and context. It was interesting that a loan could not be asked for verbally but only in writing, a fact I had noted before when members of Jon's congregation would hand him similar letters.

In West Africa, great stress is laid on verbal felicity. The man who can speak publicly with force and style is likely to rise in society as is the man who can write elegant or grammatical English or French. The form of this letter had been taken from one of the many books in Africa that offer advice on how to deal with sophisticated correspondence. As in any country where there are many languages, great social mobility and a good deal of demi-literacy, many people are unsure of what is correct or incorrect usage. Books, therefore, often offer whole letters that can be adapted for all occasions by just changing one or two words, rather like the way bad students learn whole essays by heart that they will doggedly apply to the most inappropriate circumstances in an examination. Unfortunately, the people who compile such works in Africa are far from proficient in either language or social sense and can do more harm than good.

The young are particularly a prey to scribal insecurity and a whole sub-industry provides love letters for all occasions. These are passed around between college students with a rapidity and fervour reserved in our own schools for works of dire pornography.

They contain such useful advice (from a Nigerian example) as: 'The address should be on top of the right-hand side of your pad, and you should remember that love is sweet as blue, and as such one should try to write with blue writing pad because blue always shows a deep love.'

One suggested letter runs: 'I am Jaguar Jones of Roseland. I am the queen of roses, generally respected in this land as a quiet lady but your performance has boiled my brain caused me unsteady and less working.'

In the present case, it seemed scant reward for such application and industry to simply refuse an advance. At great length, I explained that the missionary was indeed not my brother, that we were from different villages, different peoples. We did not even speak the same language. Anyway, I could not simply go about giving money to people I had never even seen before.

The scribe reeled back in outrage. His probity, he felt, had been called into question.

'Am I not an honest man?' he questioned. 'I gave you back your pen, didn't I?'

5

The Missing Mastectomy

The next morning, bright and early, I set out for the village where I had lived for some eighteen months. To either side of the road, people were cultivating in the fields and ran out to greet me. It was only with great difficulty that I avoided offers of millet beer, rotted manioc and smoked meat. By the time I reached the village, my pockets were full of eggs, benefacted upon me by Dowayos. I walked gingerly, knowing that many of them would be rotten.

Old women limped up, leaning on sticks, pinched my arms and laughed at how fat I had become. 'And you told us you had no wives . . .' they clucked roguishly, hoes tucked over their shoulders. Men came up, eyeing me hopefully for beer, ears having detected in my bag the clink of bottle against bottle.

By the time I got to the village, I was exhausted by questions, handshaking, and the minute and unashamed discussion of my person. Around the huts lay a deep silence broken only by the scratching of chickens and the humming of bees. Children peered at me round a tree and ran away giggling when I spoke to them.

I crossed the public circle and noted with surprise that the ground bore signs that the cattle had been driven into the stone enclosure at night, not simply allowed to wander promiscuously in the bush. I mentally bet that the new *sous-préfet* lay behind this habit since the Dowayos had always declared such a practice to be too onerous to be workable.

It was a moot point whether or not I had the right to enter the chief's compound uninvited. I did, after all, have a hut in there. Deciding to err rather on the side of politeness rather than familiarity, I stood at the gatehouse clapping loudly – the normal practice in much of Africa where there are no doors to knock on. There was no answer. Flies buzzed, goats belched, somewhere in the distance a woman was singing a grinding song accompanied by the dull rasp of stone on stone.

Slipping somewhat from the standards of high formality, I called out asking whether anyone was there. Still there was no answer. Giving up all claims to decent behaviour, I pushed through the gate.

The huts were all closed up, barricaded with grass mats against the incursion of dissolute goats, inquisitive little boys and – doubtless – errant anthropologists. Zuuldibo, the chief, had bought himself a fine new door made of a sheet of corrugated aluminium beaten flat. It sported a brand new Taiwanese padlock. It was locked. Few places can look as desolate as an African village without people. Mentally, I typed my report to relevant grant-giving bodies, 'The researcher visited the Dowayo people of North Cameroon to investigate their circumcision ceremony, but unfortunately they were out.'

I decided to inspect my own hut, pulling back the woven mat door and plunging into the gloomy, airless interior, assailed by a smell of goat droppings and stale flatulence. From the darkness came a rhythmic snoring – Zuuldibo.

He awoke with a start, greeted me and launched into a great description of the zeal and dedication with which he had guarded my hut in my absence. It was also, he confided, a good place to hide from the tax inspector. He had certainly made himself very much at home. The walls were covered with pictures torn from magazines depicting voluptuous ladies and large American cars. A spear lay in one corner. In the thatch were tucked little twists of cloth that doubtless contained ritually important objects such as cockerels' eggs and leopards' whiskers. Zuuldibo looked expectantly at my bag, doubtless able to detect the beer in it. I got out the two bottles. In a flash, he had whipped off the tops with the bottle-opener he carried always about his neck and sucked down a mouthful of foam with relish.

He was, he declared, glad that I had come because there were various matters that were causing him anxiety. First, there was the problem of my assistant Matthieu.

Matthieu, it seemed, had been engaging in that traditional Dowayo game – debt manipulation. In my time at the village, I had come to act very much as a banker to Zuuldibo who, like most Dowayos, was always pressed by claims for cash from relatives, taxmen, party officials, and so on. He would turn up at my hut, face averted with embarrassment – to request me to lend him some small sum which would greatly ease his present difficulties. He would always hint at vast expectations. Since, at that time, I was living in one of the huts in his compound for which no charge was made, I was always glad to help out. Zuuldibo, for his part, would always punctiliously pay back at least half before he borrowed the same sum again. I suspect that this was a familiar traditional technique for muddying the accounts. So, by slow degrees, Zuuldibo had built up a considerable debt whose precise status was left indeterminate. Was it a loan, rent – a gift? When I had returned to England, knowing that such a debt was hopelessly uncollectable, I had simply made the best of it by making a present of the whole sum to Zuuldibo in exchange for all his kindnesses to me.

This, of course, was the act of a mere beginner in Dowayo social relations. I realize now that I should simply have let the debt ride, alluding to it occasionally to keep it fresh, as the mark of our relationship. There was something inherently insulting in my zeal to clear the matter up. Rather like completely paying one's bill at the village shop, it implied a determination to close the account and so terminate the relationship.

Matthieu, however, had been made of sterner stuff and hated to see a good debt go to waste. He had determined to collect on my behalf and had badgered Zuuldibo mercilessly. Whether this had been a matter of principle or an act of personal entrepreneurship was never established. I soothed Zuuldibo, urging that I would sort out the problem with Matthieu. I did not require payment.

It seemed an opportune moment to mention the circumcision. Zuuldibo nodded. Yes, the ceremony was to happen over towards the old rain-chief's village. The boys had already been decorated in animal horns and skins and had begun to tour the area dancing at the compounds of relatives. This, finally, was a firm and definite sign that a commitment had been made to carry out the ritual and relief flooded through me. It looked as if there would soon be work to do.

Dowayo circumcision is a protected process. As in many other parts of the world, the boy is depicted as being reborn with a new name and must be taught all the attributes of culture like a small child. It begins with the decoration of the boys by the husbands of their sisters. They roam the countryside dancing and being given food at any homestead. Once the heavy rains start, the boys can be cut. The operation is designed to be terrifying. The boys are stripped naked at the crossroads and led to the riverside grove where the cutting is to be performed. On the way they are leapt upon by the circumcisers who are growling like hunting leopards and threatening them with knives. The operation is very severe, the penis being peeled for its entire length. Several different circumcisers may each cut part of the foreskin off. The boy is not supposed to cry out but old men who told me about the festival admitted that many did. It did not really matter as long as the women *thought* they were brave. At the swimming-place, one sees the result of such operations. If the operation is performed young, the penis sometimes assumes an almost spherical form that must in part be responsible for the very low birthrate of the Dowayos. Since all were cut with the same knife and the risk of infection is very great, mortality was considerable. Boys who died from the operation were said to have been eaten by leopards. From the correspondence of French colonial officers, it is clear that they were distressed by the number of youths who were said to have been eaten by leopards – although these were virtually extinct in the area. Dowayos, as a result, rapidly gained a reputation for engaging in lurid cannibalistic rites.

The boys who are circumcised must be secluded in the bush for some nine months – the same period they spend in the womb. They must avoid women. Only at the end of this period could they wander about in the wicker and leaf covering such as those I had seen. Even now they were obliged to lay down leaves to form a 'bridge' whenever they crossed over a path and to take up the polluted leaves afterwards. For freshly circumcised boys are very dangerous. They can make a pregnant woman miscarry and a young wife infertile. They must not talk to a woman directly but have little flutes with which they imitate the tone patterns of words so that they can 'talk' with music.

Only after the nine-month period may they return to the village where they are fed, dressed and shown the hearths. Later they are taken to the house where the skulls of the male ancestors are kept and see them for the first time. They are now true men and may swear oaths on their knives. (Children who do so are beaten.) It was always odd to hear men calling out the shortened version of the oath to show great rage. It comes out as 'Dang me!' Whenever I used the oath, this was felt to be highly comical.

One might wonder why circumcision is so widespread in the world and why anthropologists are apparently so obsessed with it. It might be thought that deformation of the genitals will be so painful and unpleasant that these are the last things that people would want to mutilate. When one reads of some of the customary practices relating to the sexual organs it is hard to resist the view that such mutilations are inflicted *because* they are painful. Holes may be bored in the penis. It may be regularly slashed with glass to clean it. It may be sliced open to unfold like a flower when erect. Testes may be crushed or hacked off. Nothing it seems is excluded.

Anthropologists have continued to be fascinated by such practices as part of their awareness of the sheer 'otherness' of alien peoples. If such practices can be 'explained' and related to our own ways of living then that 'otherness' has been removed and we feel we have got down to some more universal notion of what it means to be human. It would seem that if anthropological theories can cope with the sex customs, they can cope with anything.

One common 'explanation' of the widespread removal of the foreskin is that it is regarded as in some way a female element that has no place on true men.

Similar explanations have been devised to cope with the passion for excising the female clitoris – this being viewed as a residual penis that has no place on women. Culture has here been required to straighten the seams of an imperfect nature.

In my own researches with the Dowayos, although male circumcision was quite central to their culture, they would quite happily combine several such approaches at the same time. They certainly did regard circumcision as the male equivalent of menstruation. A man will, for the rest of his life, be obliged to joke with men with whom he was cut – his 'brothers of circumcision' – while a woman has to joke with the girls who began menstruating in the same year as herself – her 'sisters of menstruation'.

On the other hand, the Dowayos clearly regarded the foreskin as in some way female, complaining that uncut boys were wet, smelly, 'like women'. The Dowayos are not greatly given to involved explanations of their customs. Normally they simply explain that they do things 'because the ancestors told us to'. But here they had a ready explanation forming an interesting parallel to the local American missionaries who also circumcised their young boys and explained with great sincerity that this was done as scientifically essential for health and well-being, the foreskin being a proved source of infection and uncleanness. While the Dowayos and the Americans were equally convinced of the necessity of genital mutilation of their young, the Dowayos disapproved of the American way of going about things – firstly in that they hardly cut anything off their children and secondly that they did not keep them away from women immediately after cutting and so constituted a public-health danger.

But if circumcision is regarded as being just one way of straightening the seams of biology, there is an absent element. I have already mentioned the possibility of female circumcision. This is much publicized these days, being presented as part of a wicked plot by males to dominate females and enslave them, and therefore a subject of hot debate. The much more common mutilation of males goes unremarked.

Dowayos, however, do not mutilate female genitals. It is true that at the end of my second visit, I received a bizarre deputation of old men who had heard of such a practice and asked me to explain it to them. Once again the problem of ethics rears its head. Should the ethnographer allow himself to become involved in teaching about practices that many would regard with horror? To accept such constraints would make most of anthropology beyond the pale since most of its subject matter inspires dread in polite drawing-rooms.

We withdrew to the bush with great whispering and giggling. There, to the accompaniment of diagrams, I tried to explain the basic possibilities to a fascinated but sceptical audience. They shook their heads and pointed to the marks in the dust, amazed at the perversity of other peoples. 'But does it not hurt?' they asked, as if unaware of the agonies inflicted on boys by their own practices. 'Does it really stop women wandering about and committing adultery?' Little alternative remains in such situations to a shrug and a standard formula such as 'I do not know. I have not seen'.

Thus, the mutilation of women was at least a theoretical possibility for Dowayos. But one problem remains. In females, breasts are functional and necessary to feed the young. In males they are not. Why, therefore, do men not cut off their nipples as an intrusive female element rather than remove their foreskins? I know of no documented example anywhere in the world. Imagine, therefore, my excitement when Matthieu remarked casually that the Ninga – a neighbouring people – were odd in that their men had no nipples. I sought to confirm this statement by questioning other Dowayo men. It took some effort to work the conversation round to the topic, but they agreed that this was indeed the case. An expedition in search of the missing mastectomy was clearly in order.

6

Veni, Vidi, Visa

Matthieu arrived outside my hut the next day. He was smiling and in good heart like an old soldier called back to the ranks after years of enforced idleness. He looked bashfully at his feet. '*Patron.* I have someone outside for you.'

He led me through the courtyard, across the public square and we plunged into the long grass in a quarter of the village I had not visited before.

Suddenly, there before me stood two extremely shy, blushing youths in their circumcision outfits. They wore two long robes, one blue, one white. Buffalo horns were bound round their necks with the thick, coarse cloth that is used to wrap corpses and buy women. On their backs, they wore leopard skins stretched over wooden frames. Here there had been some element of compromise with the modern world. Leopards are now extinct in the area and the Nigerian mountains are the only current source of illegal imports of such skins at ruinous cost. One enterprising local trader has plugged the gap by importing a cotton fabric with leopard-skin markings on it. It was this that was sported by one of the youths, in place of the real skin. Knowing the Dowayos' difficulties in this area, I had brought with me a supply of leopard-skin Fablon with which English dandies are wont to ornament the insides of their cars. When I showed it to Zuuldibo, it went down very well, its stiffness and washability being deemed major advances over the natural product.

This seemed a good opportunity to try it out in the field. I sent Matthieu back to get some while the boys danced and I photographed them. It was only after some time that their musical accompanist turned up with his drum and we went through the whole thing again with the Fablon splendidly in place, the boys bending low and shaking furiously as they stamped the bells on their feet.

In accordance with Dowayo norms of hospitality, I gave one of them a small present and offered some beer. All the while, I was uncomfortably aware that in decorating either of them I had accepted new social obligations, becoming the boy's 'husband' – a relationship that lasts for life and would involve me in dressing and feeding him at the end of circumcision. In return, he would turn up to dance at my funeral.

There was a good deal of sniggering as we called each other 'wife' and 'husband' respectively.

Zuuldibo, with his uncanny beer-scenting abilities, immediately appeared and watched the boys drinking rather as a dog hovers around a child with ice-cream. His hat was a trifle askew. It was clear that he had come hot from a beer-drinking party in the fields. Having finally caught my circumcision candidates, fine specimens of about fourteen, I was loth to release them too easily and interrogated them mercilessly about their parentage, what preparations had already been made, who would be organizing the ceremony and other details. Soon they were yawning pitiably, leaning against each other and demanding sleep. Zuuldibo, moreover, had decided that this was the best time to address the problem of the roof of my hut. He was not to be put off.

The roof, he observed, spreading himself easily on the ground and breaking wind – a friendly mark that we were in all-male company and could discourse freely – had been a very fine roof. He himself had supervised the thatching of it because I was his friend. I could not resist interjecting that it had leaked badly from the start but Zuuldibo waved this remark aside. The boys dozed. We were obviously to suffer a prepared speech. The roof, Zuuldibo asserted, had been remarkably fine and much admired. It had been fitting for a man of wealth such as myself. But now it was leaking. Zuuldibo suffered when he was inside guarding the hut. He was glad to suffer for me, his friend, without payment, but I would need a new roof. How much would it cost? It was, he felt, unseemly to discuss such matters. Zuuldibo would take upon himself the execution of necessary works. He would ensure it was well done. I would give him what I felt was proper reward for the heavy sufferings of the workers.

This is a frequent ploy to stop haggling, shame often driving the buyer to offer far more than he would otherwise be prepared to pay. Zuuldibo was obviously in his cups or he would clearly see that he was leaving himself open to the most straightforward debt-bandying. Zuuldibo owed me money. I would owe Zuuldibo money. When he asked for payment for the roof, I could simply annul his debt and leave him to face the workers. It was an attractive idea but I knew I could never do it. My own notions of responsibility and shame would prevent it. I would feel guilt every time I saw the men and they looked disappointed.

The anthropologist is a great nuisance in any village, constantly harassing innocent people with trying questions. He draws heavily upon reserves of patience and good will. It is unreasonable for him to refuse to make some small contribution to the community in which he lives. Thatching is, moreover, a very unpleasant job whose discomforts had been only marginally overstated by Zuuldibo.

The English notion of the thatcher deriving rural satisfaction from the leisurely toil of skilled hands bears little relationship to the task of covering an African roof. The grass used emits huge quantities of suffocating pollen, causing appalling rashes and choking fits. After a day's work, thatchers would often be found gasping for breath, broiling in the hot sun. The associations of the job are closer to those of coal-mining than weaving.

I agreed that Zuuldibo and I could discuss the price later, knowing, of course, that the work would never be done before I left but that I would still have to pay for it.

Zuuldibo waxed ebullient. Beer was called for, a small furtive boy being sent to secure supplies from wife number two. He leaned back under a tree and warmed to his theme. He had, it seemed, also been giving thought to his own status. It was assumed, naturally, that he would be accompanying me to all festivals concerned with circumcision. The difficulty lay in his umbrella.

Traditionally, the chiefs of West Africa are shaded by red umbrellas. Sometimes, these become regalia of great artistic elaboration and are much ornamented and embellished with rare vehemence. Zuuldibo had settled for a much less complex expedient and bought a red ladies' umbrella made in Hong Kong. In illustration of his point, he drew it forth from beneath his robes, erected it and assumed an expression of extreme idiocy, tongue lolling out of his mouth, eyes wild. Everyone laughed. I could see what he meant.

Zuuldibo was aware that an immaculate umbrella is a rare thing but a raddled one a mere comic prop. His umbrella had never been one of the finest. Its fabric was ripped and stained by a hundred chance misfortunes that seemed to be largely associated with beer. Bare ribs poked spokily forth like orphans' arms. The stem was bent.

Zuuldibo needed a new umbrella otherwise how could he be seen at festivals? I agreed to look for one at the first opportunity. Zuuldibo

leaned forth eagerly. The chief of Marko had an umbrella with a
... there followed a lengthy interlude of linguistic discussion in
which we finally pinned down the Dowayo word for 'tassel'. Could
he have one too? I would try. If at all possible, if God wished it, he
would have his tassel. Zuuldibo beamed. My 'wife' left, promising
to send word when the ceremony would take place. The beer
arrived, accompanied by two of Zuuldibo's brothers.

Being punctilious in matters of etiquette, Zuuldibo poured a
healthy draught of the turgid, bubbling liquid into a calabash and
took a single matronly sip to show that nothing detrimental to the
well-being of his guests was intended. He then proffered it to myself.
Possibly I was infected by his own courtliness. Whatever the reason,
instead of simply draining the cup as would have been expected, I
held it up and proclaimed Zuuldibo's name in a toast. Immediately,
a deep and shocked silence descended upon the gathering. The boys
stopped talking. Zuuldibo's smile froze upon his face. The very flies
seemed hushed from their buzzing. I knew, as everyone knows who
works in an alien culture, that I had made a serious mistake.

The problem lies in the fact that the Dowayos have no notion of
our institution of 'toasting'. All they have is an institution of
cursing. When wronged beyond human bearing a man may curse
another by calling out his name, sipping beer and spitting the
contents of his mouth on to the earth. It is then expected that the
victim will weaken and die, especially if he is in a relation of
dependence to the man who has cursed him, for example, if he is
his son.

Zuuldibo and the others sat, watching horrified, waiting for me
to spit. What wrong could have led to such a vile act on my part?

I smiled in what I hoped desperately was a disarming fashion
and tried to explain. There was a sudden relaxing of tension.
Our roles were immediately, ridiculously, reversed – Zuuldibo the
ethnographer, me the confused and hopeless informant.

'We do this in my village,' I explained, 'to show that we wish the man we name long life and many wives and children. It is a custom of my people.'

He frowned, 'But how can your words make a man live long?'

'No. It's not quite like that. We just show it is our wish – that we are friends.'

'But this means that the other men there – that you do not name – you wish them to die, their wives to have no children?'

'No. You don't understand.' An inspiration. 'It's like the opposite of cursing. It means good things.'

'Ahh.'

It was the famed 'comparative method' of anthropology in action, an enlightening example of a way in which we both had half a picture that was meaningless until put together. I was also discomfortingly aware of how Zuuldibo had forced my thought into paths that were not their own. Until I discussed it with him, I had no clear thoughts at all about toasting, about why we did it, what we expected its effects to be. It was very disconcerting.

The boys rose and pattered away lightly down the path, being soon swallowed up by the tall grass, the jangling bells around their ankles coming back in waves. Abruptly a new sound took over. It was a motorbike, a *suzukiyo* in Dowayo. The arrival of a motorbike in the village is not an everyday occurrence and we all rushed down to the cactus hedge around the village to see who it was. The sound died away as the machine descended into a dip. Then, astride a wildly bucking machine, there appeared a gendarme with an automatic carbine slung over his back. Zuuldibo and I looked at each other in unspoken recognition of the fact that he had come for one of us. Swiftly, he folded his comic umbrella and slipped away, knees bent like Groucho Marx lest his head appear above the hedge. It seemed I stood alone. People fled in all directions, rather as if a visit by Attila the Hun had been announced. There followed a pause while the gendarme parked his bike and threatened various forms of physical dismemberment to the crowd of children if they touched his machine. He appeared somewhat diffidently in the gateway, dropped his carbine and shook hands with me. To my relief I recognized him as one of the pleasant idlers from the police post. As we entered my hut, I had a moment's dread of finding Zuuldibo there but it was empty. 'Where is everyone?' he asked in French.

'Oh, they must be in the fields.'

'Is the chief here?'

'I think he had to go off.'

'Well, it's you I'm here for anyway. But the captain says we must always greet the local chief before we enter the village.'

He pulled out a letter, embossed with stamps and numerals. Inside was a flimsy piece of paper bearing the word 'Convocation'. It was a complete mystery to me.

'Er, what does it mean?' The gendarme gave me a pitying look.

'You have to go to the prefect's office in Garoua at once. I expect it means you're being deported.'

He smiled beatifically. It was clearly going to be one of those days. Fieldwork seems to consist of long periods that are impossible to reconstruct afterwards because nothing happened, alternating with days of intense activity when one rides a rollercoaster of good fortune and disaster.

I offered him a beer – the very last of my stock – and tried to find out more. It was useless, he did not know any more but was delighted to take off his boots, ease his feet and question me about the Dowayos rather like a good British bobby informing himself about his 'patch'. Today everyone was an anthropologist. Being a Southerner, he engaged in a good deal of headshaking about 'primitive ways' and insisted I write down an account of his own circumcision in the forests of that area. He laid great stress upon the fact that at marriage his wife had been obliged to pay him one franc – 'for the pain of circumcision he had suffered that he might give her joy'.

Having finally found a desperately keen informant, albeit one from entirely the wrong area, it was dispiriting to have to work the conversation round to more mundane matters. The convocation?

The message had come over the radio this morning and the captain had sent him out to find me. He looked coy and regarded his feet with rapt attention. He could, of course, always tell the captain I had been away in the bush so that he had been forced to leave a note on my door. This would give me time to see the *sous-préfet* before the police got hold of me. He would even give me a lift into town on the back of his motorbike if I would promise to jump off and hide if anyone came the other way.

We left to much twitching of grass mats, eyes peering out from behind them like genteel ladies keeping watch behind net curtains. Outside the town, I was dropped off.

My visit was quite astonishingly uncomplicated. The *sous-préfet* was at home, free and willing to see me. He waved me inside and listened to my story. My passport was inspected. After a swift perusal, he stabbed it with his finger. 'Here is the trouble. They gave you a provisional visa in the capital, not a temporary one.' There indeed was the visa, a head with an insulting caricature of the profile of an African woman. Inevitably, I thought of Precocious and his hideous ivory pendants. Beside it, were stamped the doom-laden words 'valid for three weeks, non-renewable'. With a deft hand, the *sous-préfet* simply deleted the non-renewable clause and stamped it. 'You had better go to Garoua,' he urged. 'I will write you a note to the prefect.'

I stammered out suitable thanks. 'Do not mention it. Another thing. My car has to go to the city tomorrow morning. If you like, there is no reason why you cannot sit in it.'

So, far from being shipped off in chains as I had imagined, I ended up being chauffeur-driven. Such violent alternations of fortune work powerfully upon the mind. Anthropologists are perhaps distinguished by possessing a supplementary gear into which they can drop in the face of frustration and disaster. It is a state almost of suspended animation, devoid of emotion, in which the most fearful misfortunes or accretions of minor irritations simply wash over the fieldworker in a way that would astonish friends and relations at home who may know the person concerned as energetic and incisive.

As I sped by in a sea of equanimity, policemen at the roadside saluted me. I was spared the usual document checks. Inevitably in such situations one remembers childhood stories of the complacent speeding to their doom carrying the warrants for their own execution. By the time we reached the city, however, I had all but perfected the magisterial wave of huge condescension bestowed upon those who witnessed my passage. I had begun to feel that maybe I had got the hang of African bureaucracies.

The prefect's office struck back in relatively muted fashion. The note from the *sous-préfet* aroused a certain amount of suspicion. It was handled with great circumspection as if it might turn out to be important evidence against me. 'What is your connection with the *sous-préfet*?' asked one hostile official. 'He married my sister.' The official nodded sagaciously. Soon my passport sported a new visa in defiance of the non-renewable clause. The official smiled. 'There is one problem. You need a 200-franc fiscal stamp.' He shrugged. 'We have none. There are no 200-franc fiscal stamps in the city.' He leaned forward. 'If you meet me behind the building in ten minutes, I may be able to help. Otherwise you can wait in Garoua till we get some.' His exaggerated use of mouth and eyebrows suggested this would not be a wise move.

I withdrew and loitered with studied innocence outside the door then slipped behind the building.

Here, furtively, we kept our tryst. The upshot of it all was that I ended up buying a 200-franc stamp for 400 francs. As I left, he asked again, 'Is he really married to your sister?' I looked wide-eyed with wonder. 'Of course.'

It was time to sort out accommodation for the night and I made, as usual, for a small hotel that consisted of a clutch of cement huts, but with running water. It sat next to the brand-new, self-consciously grand Novotel, across from the city too. At all hours of the day and night, air-conditioned buses carried up loads of French and German tourists in Yves Saint-Laurent safari suits.

7

Of Simians and Cinemas

It is important in this world to know to whom one is attractive. There was once a particularly touching advertisement for mosquito repellent that began, 'One person in two thousand is naturally unattractive to mosquitoes'. Alas, sitting on the terrace of the small hotel in Garoua, it was painfully clear that I did not fall into that category. The mosquitoes of that city are determined and vicious, taking time off from relentless procreation only to savage hapless humans. When the doughty female explorer Olive McLeod visited the city just after the turn of the century and had dinner with the German governor, liveried servants placed a domesticated toad at the side of each of the guests to lessen the ravages of the blood-sucking insects.

But mosquitoes do not exhaust my charm. I have a yet stronger effect on monkeys. In England, this attraction remains latent. In Africa, it comes to the fore.

In Dowayoland, I had encountered baboons, possibly the least lovely of simians. Troops of them lived a vocal and arid existence in the rocks beside the path that led to the rain-chief's domain. As I crawled along that sickeningly precipitous track, they would scream and gibber at me and occasionally throw rocks. I suspect now, however, that what I took for rage and aggression was merely a manifestation of frustrated love.

My next encounter with a baboon was when seated on a rock in the middle of a river. In the environs of Ngaoundere was a pleasant spot where the river dropped a clear fifty or sixty feet in a beautiful waterfall. The air was always cool and full of rainbows and dragonflies. A conveniently situated rock made a fine place to sit and bask.

As I sat and contemplated the beauties of nature, I was approached by a baboon. It sat and regarded me with obvious interest from the river bank, exploring its body for fleas in a most immodest fashion. Soon a certain sympathy had developed between us and it daintily picked its way on all fours to where I sat and stared fixedly into my face as if hoping to find I was a long-lost relative. Suddenly it yawned and apparently pointed to something over my head. So great was the sympathy between us that it never occurred to me that this was not a gesture intended for me and I turned round to see what was being pointed at. The baboon, profiting from my distraction, seized my left nipple through the open shirt and began sucking on it vigorously. It did not take this sagacious beast long to realize that this was a fruitless endeavour and we withdrew in mutual embarrassment, the baboon going so far as to spit most offensively. It is possible that this incident was in part responsible for the idea of the missing mastectomy and attendant events. These I shall relate later.

As I sat on the terrace, quietly swatting mosquitoes, I saw an old friend, Bob, a black American anthropologist. We shared a beer and caught up with each other's news. But out of the corner of my eye, I spotted a movement, at once strange and familiar. It was a monkey swinging through the trees. I knew it was coming for me.

It turned out subsequently that the local zoo had two baby monkeys. I do not know what kind they were, apes, chimpanzees, gorillas, they are all my children. The female of the pair had died. The male had been plunged into deepest mourning. Being an intelligent creature, it had noted that the padlock of its cage was defective. The keeper, in accordance with the regulations that governed his endeavours, had applied in triplicate to the capital for a new padlock. No answer had been received. Any manner of fastening the cage that resisted the monkey's overnight attempts to open it, proved too onerous and inconvenient for the keeper. Any less final form of closure enabled the monkey to undo the fastening and wander at will during hours of darkness. But it always returned to its cage by morning, the only home it had ever known. A standing arrangement had evolved to the mutual satisfaction of both parties.

In return for being available for public inspection during the day, the monkey was now permitted to engage in nocturnal excursions that had greatly improved its morale. Each evening, it would patiently undo the lock on its door, swing itself into the trees and embark upon a search for suitable company. It has to be confessed that it had sometimes abused this privilege through high spirits but had never failed to report for work in the morning. One of its favourite haunts was the swimming pool of the luxury hotel next door. It delighted in insinuating itself into the changing-huts, plundering the clothes there and retiring to the safety of the trees.

There it would explore the wallets and purses of foreign tourists, raining money, travel documents and doubtless private secrets on the heads of those below, immune to their cries and cajoleries. This had now become an important source of income for the hotel workers who therefore encouraged its visits.

After a moment spent contemplating me from a tree, it dropped to the ground, trotted over to our table and stared at me with the utmost gravity. Over the wall dividing the two establishments drifted howls of rage. Clearly it had just carried out a particularly vehement visitation.

Spotting it, a waiter immediately rushed over to hit it on the head with a rock. This represents a fairly standard Cameroonian

66

response to wildlife. Knowingly, it slid both arms around my neck and slid into my lap, baring green, horribly fetid teeth at its tormentor. Only with the utmost difficulty did I persuade the waiter that it was more reasonable not to hit the monkey – now firmly clamped to me like a limpet mine – so that it would surely savage me nastily, but rather to seek to lure it away with a dish of peanuts. Scowling and muttering, the waiter finally complied, making it abundantly clear that a charge would be made for the nuts. The monkey, however, was not to be parted from me. It began to snore, breathing rank halitosis in my face, disdaining proffered treats. Well-meaning attempts to disentangle its arms produced enraged barks and baring of surely rabid fangs. Stroking its head brought sighs and grunts of such deep sadness that it would have taken a stonier heart than my own to even seek to discard the beast.

The problem was that Bob and I had set our hearts on a visit to the cinema. Cinemas do not loom large in the accounts of anthropologists yet they are curiously important when in the field. Normally totally inaccessible, they become a focus for feelings of deprivation and nostalgia. Whenever in a town, they must be visited. It does not matter that one knows in advance that the film will be terrible, the soundtrack incomprehensible, the experience full of heat and dust and sweat. It must be done nevertheless. And in town there was a new wonder. An entirely new picture palace had just been opened. It even had seats and a roof. Air-conditioning was promised at any moment. This very evening was one when the film, though doubtless far from new, was not a Kung Fu spectacular or a Muslim epic concerned with the monumental slaying of unbelievers.

Life is full of those actions that seem perfectly reasonable at the time. The logic of a situation is a purely local thing. Many actions, when looked back upon, seem bizarre and inexplicable. 'Why don't we just take him along?' suggested Bob. At that particular moment, nothing seemed more natural than that I should take the snoring simian along to the cinema with me. A few tentatively exploratory movements revealed that motion was permitted as long as one hand was kept free to caress the beast. Otherwise, there was more baring of teeth and snarling. It required only slightly more dexterity than that of the average contortionist to insinuate myself into a jacket not designed for a man wearing a monkey and to button it up over the creature. In the damp heat of the evening I felt very warm indeed. Good fortune had provided me with a truck borrowed from my long-suffering friends at the mission. We set off for the cinema, an oddly assorted trio.

It would be nice to be able to report that the film on offer was *King Kong* but it was, I fear, a rather indifferent American comedy about divorce that seemed to fall rather flat among polygamous Muslims.

We queued at the ticket office, various members of the public eyeing my snoring paunch with suspicion. To my great distress, the monkey was detected by the fiery ticket-seller who flared her nostrils at me and called the French manager. I fully expected this to be the end of the matter. The manager would avail himself of the opportunity to vent Gallic rage and point out with ruthless logic all the perfectly valid reasons why simians were not admitted. We should then be shown the door.

Surprisingly, the central issue seemed not to be the admissibility of simians but rather what sort of ticket they required. Bob entered into the spirit of the thing and declared the monkey to be clearly a 'minor' and therefore entitled to a reduction. It would not even be occupying a seat. The manager was unwilling to concede the point, fearing perhaps the setting of a precedent. Did he really foresee a stream of people with lions and ant-eaters, refusing payment on this slim pretext? In the end it was agreed that the monkey would be charged at half the rate of the cheapest seat and that we would sit in the least elegant part of the house. I paid up. The monkey slipped back under the coat and began to snore again.

The first part of the programme was not popular. It consisted of a luridly verbose travelogue about holiday cruises in the West Indies. As usual, there were few barriers between members of the audience and conventions of strict silence were certainly not observed. The gentleman beside me, having removed his shoes to ease large splayed feet and unbuttoned his immaculate military uniform to the navel, joked lengthily and repeatedly about my ancestors having given his ancestors free passage on such ships during the slave trade. Bob, a self-aware black American, took such remarks rather ill and a definite atmosphere of tension developed between himself and the military man.

It was at this point that the much-vaunted air-conditioning seemed to leap into action. The temperature dropped steadily until there was a definite chill in the air. It seemed to become more and more hyperactive. Instead of merely mitigating the oppressive heat, it declared war on it. Jets of icy air belched into the room. A sort of miasmic fog seemed to form beneath the screen as the bland French voice prattled on about 'getting away from the cold this winter' on a Caribbean cruise.

The military gentleman began buttoning his uniform and struggling back into his boots. Worse yet, the sudden chill penetrated to my simian friend and he poked forth his head to the considerable distress of the lady behind. It was unfortunate that she owned a large, red, shiny handbag. The monkey wanted that handbag desperately and was enraged at the lady's dogged refusal to yield it up. In an attempt to distract the monkey, I bought it a large, red, shiny mango from a passing vendor. Mangoes, however, were strange and unnatural to it. Whatever its normal fare, mangoes were clearly no part of it.

The monkey limited itself to biting the mango into strips and spitting it at members of the audience. Its range was surprisingly great. Bored by the film, they took this in good part, promptly purchased mangoes and began spitting them back at the monkey and – inevitably – at me. The manager, alerted by minions fearful for the décor, hurried up and began threatening eviction. The audience settled back to enjoy a good row as the news came on.

The big story seemed to be a meeting between the President and some unidentifiable Chinese minister dispensing aid. There was the inevitable scene of the President executing a waxy smile into the camera, eyes awkwardly fixed on the lens as he offered the visitor one of the hideous plastic armchairs that always featured in such scenes. 'He should use the aid to buy some new furniture,' opined the military man in a loud voice. The audience roared, the news erupted into the national anthem, half the spectators rose, the other half made noises. It was all too much for the monkey. Sated with society, he began to gibber and scream. The audience liked that too. The background of the national anthem made our behaviour dangerously close to lèse-majesté. It was the moment to leave, the main film unseen. In a St Peter-like act of perfidy, Bob remained behind.

We drove back in silence. As I climbed out in front of the hotel, the monkey slipped fluidly to the ground and looked at me a final time as if wondering whether an embrace was too bold on a first date. Deciding against further displays of affection, he shambled off across the yard and swung back into the trees, heading for the zoo.

After all the excitement, I felt quite tired and did not in the least mind missing the main feature at the cinema. However, I did not sleep very well. I had fleas – monkey fleas.

8

When in Doubt – Charge!

Back in Poli, all was quiet. At the mission there was a brooding silence. Jon's crops had been ravaged by unidentified beasts. The town chief's cattle were deeply suspected. Somehow, I felt sure it was baboons. Had Jon's wife been a Dowayo lady, she would have expected to be beaten for adultery – the inevitable cause of damage to a man's crops.

In the village, Zuuldibo, when unearthed from under my bed, proclaimed that preparations were continuing for the circumcision but that nothing interesting could happen for some time yet. I knew from previous experience, that it was the brewing of the beer that would be the real point of no return. When I heard that it was brewing, I would know that the time had come. Just to make sure, I sent Matthieu over to the village where it was to be held with a present of tobacco for one of his relatives who lived there. They would be sure to send word in good time.

In the interim, there was plenty to keep me occupied since I had started studying local healers and their remedies. But since I could reasonably count on a few weeks' respite, I determined to carry out the mission that might constitute my only major contribution to anthropology. I would visit the Ninga to search for the ritual removal of male breasts – the missing mastectomy that had been mentioned by my Dowayo informants.

It was clear from the outset that Matthieu did not want to go to the Ninga. The paths were dangerous, he assured me. There would be no one there at this time of the year. No one spoke their language. They would not talk to me. They were bad people.

It is one of the more depressing discoveries of the anthropologist that almost all peoples loathe, fear and despise the people next door.

From one of the male nurses at the hospital, I had learned that the chief of the Ninga was in Poli and resolved to track him down. It took hours of wandering round the outlying huts. Once again, it was clear to everyone what a white man wanted despite his protestations and pathetic pretences. I had not previously realized that commercial vice existed as such in such a small town. But exist it certainly did and I was tirelessly offered most of it. There was also an awkward encounter with a member of the police who emerged from one compound in a dishevelled state and explained with great insistence that he was investigating illegal drinking.

It was only at nightfall, tired, hot and deeply resentful, that I finally discovered the chief of the Ninga, being beckoned into his presence by an urchin I had hired as a guide. Clearly his avoidance techniques were every bit as good as Zuuldibo's. The chief was a dwarf, clothed entirely in a bright red robe of thick flannel rather like Father Christmas's assistants. From under the robe, peeked out saucily the toes of glossy white shoes. As I entered his compound, he rushed at me rather like an over-enthusiastic terrier, hugged me fiercely, burying his face in my stomach and declared his joy at seeing me.

We seated ourselves on two upturned crates and we began our audience, the urchin acting as interpreter. I announced my delight at seeing the chief and explained my mission in these parts was to study 'customs'. He nodded sagely. I had heard many interesting things about the Ninga and my heart longed to visit him in his village to learn about Ninga ways. On the whole this approach seemed preferable to simply saying, 'Look, about male nipples . . .'

He smiled benevolently at the translation of my words. He had heard of me among the Dowayos – always his friends. His heart yearned to take me to his village. He would gladly discuss with me Ninga ways. He had heard that I was a man of straight words. He looked coy. There was only one problem. He was a poor man. He could not entertain me as I would wish. Yet he was proud. He could not bear to receive me and disappoint my expectations. He sighed. There was only one way round it. I would have to buy a goat. A thousand francs would be quite sufficient. I might as well pass over the money now. I baulked. This was as straightforward a demand for cash as I had ever encountered. It was difficult to know whether this was a moment appropriate to no-nonsense, man-to-man toughness or to spontaneous generosity devoid of haggling. Anthropology, alas, requires always a measure of hypocrisy and calculation. A swift check of my pockets revealed a total of some 500 francs so generosity was out.

Alas, I explained, I too was a poor man. Not being a chief, I was unaccustomed to eating whole goats, so I would give the chief the price of half a goat – 500 francs. He looked very disappointed. Having come so far and discovered a phenomenon as vital as the excision of male nipples, it seemed ridiculous to haggle over slightly more than a pound. Somehow, this was an argument I always used on myself before giving in. I added that I would, of course, expect to give the chief a present when I visited him. 'A guest does not come with empty hands.'

The chief brightened visibly and we agreed that in a week's time our urchin interpreter would come to the village to fetch me and we would climb the mountain together. As I sought to leave, the chief again made a rush at me, clutching my unresisting form to himself. He seized my hand and clasped it passionately to his heart. 'White men and black men', he observed, 'are brothers. It is just that white men are cleverer.'

It was difficult to know quite how to respond to that. Having just been parted from all my money, I did not feel particularly clever, so we let the matter lie. 'Do not linger too long in these areas,' he solemnly warned. 'Here there are many bad women.' I began to guess where my 500 francs would end up.

Nine days later, there had been no further sign from the chief of the Ninga. African notions of time are somewhat looser than our own. I remembered with embarrassment the arrival of the Dowayo rain-chief the day *after* my farewell party in the bland expectation that drink would have been kept for him.

Still, it looked as though a visit to the chief of the nippleless Ninga would not go amiss. I set off with Matthieu as soon as it got light – he predicting doom as usual. Once more we had to go through a great deal of wandering about. In polygynous households there is often a nomadic element in sleeping arrangements. People were crouched around fires, clutching blankets to themselves in the early morning chill, waiting for food or warm beer. Great expectorations resounded on all sides.

The house of the chief was empty. No one knew where he was. No one knew when he would return. Matthieu explained that this was because they were all bad people. I decided to try my nurse informant at the hospital.

Since this involved passing directly in front of the *sous-préfet*'s house, a courtesy visit would be necessary there also.

The compact figure of the *sous-préfet* was already crouched over his desk, a stack of papers spread out before him. As we shook hands, a broad grin spread over his face. He waved a piece of paper in the air. 'Aha. I have a report about you from the police. Apparently, you have been visiting a lady of the night.'

The more I denied it, the more he delightedly refused to believe anything but the worst of me. We finally got round to the question of the chief of the Ninga. 'The chief of the Ninga? But I can tell you

74

where he is.' He leaned back in his chair and assumed his most cherubic expression. 'I sent him back to his village. He is a bad example, lying around in town, drinking, fornicating. How are young men to respect their chiefs with such behaviour? I have sent him back to collect the tax properly.' He waved a reproachful finger at me. 'You had better behave *yourself* or I will be sending you back to *yours*.'

The conversation got round to the subject of circumcision. The *sous-préfet*'s approach was plagued by all the unresolved discomforts of any administrator from one culture who rules over members of another. As a Muslim, he, of course, regarded circumcision as a good thing in itself. It was inherently civilizing and was therefore to be encouraged among the pagans. He was aware, however, that it was disruptive, dangerous and expensive. He was therefore in the habit of sending out the male nurses to perform the operation in the villages, instead of letting the local people do it, 'with a dirty hoe'. They were at least more moderate in their excisions and relatively hygienic, though the stipulation that all wounds be doused in alcohol must have greatly increased the pain involved. What the *sous-préfet* did not know was that some of the elders, dissatisfied with this arrangement, circumcised the boys a second time once the nurses had left: humanitarian measures of a good administrator had thus greatly increased the pain, suffering and mortality of the boys – in the best traditions of colonial rule.

It was during this talk that I first heard of the water project that was to prove a major problem of the future. The *sous-préfet*, in collaboration with the American Peace Corps, had determined that the town needed a pure water supply. As I walked back to my village, I little realized what a tangled issue this would become. I was more interested in my search for the missing mastectomy.

One of the principles of the British Army has always been, 'When in doubt – Charge!' It seemed the moment to apply it to my own fieldwork. Zuuldibo confirmed that several men in the village knew the paths to the Ninga which involved dangerous climbing. He would send me one who was strong, intelligent, honest and so on. I resolved to leave at first light for the Ninga. Matthieu was much displeased. If Ninga in town had been bad enough, Ninga up a mountain were even worse. 'It is the wrong season to climb the mountain,' he declared. 'It will rain. We shall be washed off. There will be no drinking-water.'

The next morning, before daybreak, there was a polite coughing outside my hut too genteel to be that of a goat. Outside stood a shivering waif in torn shorts and a magnificent red Beatles hat. In his hand, he bore a pet bird of many colours, not a parrot but rather resembling a kingfisher. It was the guide Zuuldibo had sent – a boy of about eight. We drank coffee and sat on the cold rocks talking. It appeared that the boy's mother was Ninga – married to a Dowayo man – and that he had served on a number of cattle drives from the high plateau to the valley. His knowledge was not to be called into question. With some difficulty Matthieu was roused. An hour later, we set off with camera, notebooks, tobacco – all the standard elements of the ethnographic trade.

Our guide sat his bright bird on his hat as a gage and set off in front. Matthieu trailed gloomily behind, complaining of the inadequacy of his breakfast.

Thick bands of woolly fog rolled across the valley floor. We squelched our way through mud and broken rocks to the base of the mountain range. Startled cattle would suddenly loom up out of the mist and crash off snorting into the long grass. It was bitterly cold and we all scanned the horizon hoping the weak rays of the sun would soon break through and warm us. The pet bird puffed up its feathers and essayed a faint chirp or two.

After half an hour, we met a party bound for a funeral beyond

Kongle. They bore bubbling pots of beer and dry, crackling cattle-skins to wrap the corpse and were clearly in high good spirits at the prospect of meat from the cattle that would be slaughtered. I was glad that Zuuldibo had not come with us. He would never have allowed the beer to pass untasted. The 'mourners' made cheerful jokes about my constant attendance, vulture-like, at Dowayo funerals. We exchanged tobacco for mountain bananas and they went on their way puffing happily – the cigarettes being rolled in a page of my notebook. Our little guide fed some banana to his bird, set it back on his cap at a festive tilt and we began to climb.

The climb is not pleasant. The path is often very narrow, its thin, crumbly edges sloping down towards the rocks below. When wet, the granite is very slippery and unforgiving towards anyone who loses his footing. As we climbed , drops of heavy dew slithered coldly down our necks and arms whenever we touched the vegetation that sprouted rankly in the crevices. Soon, we came upon a deep cleft littered with broken bottles and smashed calabashes. Our small guide paused here and pointed it out as a place where dwelt a strong spirit of the earth and urged us to make an offering of any food we were carrying. I gave up a banana and a piece of chocolate, Matthieu somewhat grudgingly yielded up a pinch of instant coffee and some smoked meat that he had secreted in the bottom of his pack against contingencies. Our guide nodded approvingly and set off again, the bird bobbing and shuffling as he heaved himself over the rocks. Soon flies came to torment us, feeding on our sweat and running infuriatingly in and out of our eyes. The sun grew hotter and hotter. Out of breath, miserable from the flies and bruises, I amazed my companions by insisting on a rest.

Such was not to be had, however. This was a path used by cattle. The bones of some of the less sure-footed were pointed out to encourage me on one of the more difficult stretches. Something about the altitude seemed to have stimulated the ruminant bovines to defecation. Everywhere lay cowpats with feasting flies that soon made manifest their preference for our own secretions. The sun was by now very hot and it was as well to be off.

Matthieu railed against the cowpats as another proof of the vileness of Ninga ways. When they came down to the Valley they left cattle-dung all over the Dowayos' fields. This, he affirmed, made the weeds grow and therefore greatly increased the hardships of cultivation.

I began to feel that he was a hostile witness.

Some time later, we came to the outskirts of a village. When you approach a village in West Africa, there are normally certain infallible signs. First, you come across the fields. Often there is a resonant thud of pestle in mortar as women remove the husks from the grain or their unaccompanied song as they grind it with stones. Inevitably, there are children running and shouting. More often than not there is laughter. From this village came only deep silence.

It soon became clear that some demographic disaster had befallen the village. When compounds become empty, they are normally abandoned. Under the tropical rains, the mud from which they are made soon reverts to nature, leaving nothing but the poignant circles of stones that served as foundations for the huts or granaries. This is very sad for archaeologists and a great happiness to ecologists. Here, the whole village seemed to consist of crumbling compounds. In a very few years, there would be nothing here to mark the spot where whole families had lived and died. We picked our way through this desolation towards the centre and settled on a dry-stone wall while our diminutive guide went off to seek our reluctant host.

Matthieu took advantage of the considerable delay that followed to favour me with a lengthy account of the many points he had noted during our journey that reinforced his negative assessment of these people. Where were they all? What had happened to them?

God had clearly punished them, on account of their wicked ways. He announced his verdict with considerable satisfaction. They had left this bad place. They were now being bad people elsewhere.

Finally, the chief appeared, his arrival presaged by a rhythmic thudding. This was not the accompaniment of a drumming praise-singer, as I had at first supposed. How was it that I had not noticed before that he had a club foot that made him limp? The climb up the mountain must have been sheer agony to him.

Despite his physical handicap, he made another terrier-like rush at me that nearly knocked me off the wall. He clutched my hand to his bosom and crooned his delight at my coming. As I struggled to my feet, I saw Matthieu out of the corner of my eye, mouthing distaste. Two bottles of shop-bought beer were produced. After a little pantomime between Matthieu and myself as to whether we should share a bottle, a third bottle was summoned forth and was given, to the chief's visible distress, to Matthieu. In terms of the amount of human suffering that had gone into making it available in that place at that time, it must have been one of the most costly bottles on earth.

The chief explained that he had been forced to return by press of public duties; moreover he had dreamed that one of his wives was ill and concern for her well-being had overridden the demands of good manners. I nodded agreement. He would assign a hut to Matthieu and myself and we should meet later in the evening when I had rested. There was just one small problem. I had paid for half a goat when we had met in the town. It was impossible, however, to kill just half a goat. Could I perhaps see my way clear to paying for the other half? Then no charge would be made for the use of the hut.

I paid up as Matthieu shook his head and muttered about 'bad people'.

The hut we were assigned was one of the most wretched I ever saw. The roof beams, eaten away by termites on one side, had collapsed and the whole rotting thatch hung down over the walls, leaving the other side bare. I hoped it would not rain. Our young guide made his farewells, but promised to return later that day to act as interpreter. 'Before you go,' I asked, 'how many Ninga are there?' He paused and went through elaborate calculations, involving much staring at the heavens. He smiled. 'Twenty-six!' Leaving me somewhat taken aback, he tucked up his bird inside his hat, replaced it on his head and set off for his mother's people.

I suppose I should have thought to ask the question before but from the way the Dowayos spoke of them, I had assumed that the Ninga were a people rather after the fashion of the Dowayos themselves. No one had ever thought to mention that there were so few of them.

When I questioned him about it later, the chief was a little vague as to what had happened to his people, as if they had only been mislaid. In the past they had been more numerous. There had been disease. Some had moved following a disagreement. Some had intermarried with other peoples. Fulani families had installed themselves around the Ninga to take advantage of the dry-season grazing for there was always water up the mountain. Many of the empty compounds we had seen belonged to Fulani who were away with their cattle. It seemed that in a very few years, the Ninga would be no more.

This all came as rather a blow. It is true that some of the peoples studied by anthropologists in South America are scarcely more numerous. Disease, dispossession and warfare have reduced them to tiny fragments of their former selves. To work on a people as depleted as this would be as much a work of archaeology as of anthropology. Given the importance of the missing mastectomy, it was as well that I was there at such a critical moment. For when a people loses its identity what the anthropologist regrets most is

1 Poli main street. Although it appears on even large-scale maps as a comfortingly large town with petrol, a *sous-préfecture* and an airstrip, the first sight of the main street can be uninspiring. Poli has much of the air of a Wild West frontier town. Even the main street is a dead end, running out amongst rank weeds and a failed garage.

2 Dowayoland: the Dowayo area of North Cameroon. The granite mountains rise to a height of some 5,000 feet. With their rocky outcrops, they provided shelter from raids by the equestrian Fulani. The elevation is sufficient to give a much cooler climate than on the baking plains below and allow the cultivation of superior forms of millet. The difficulties of travel in such terrain account for the preservation of much of the traditional Dowayo lifestyle.

3 The village of Kongle. Huts are made of dried mud with thatched roofs that blend into the landscape. They are surrounded by a palisade or cactus hedge. The spikes on the roofs are protection against the activities of witches.

4 In return for hospitality, the author commissioned a new hut (price £14). Dowayos held it as inappropriate for a European to live in a round hut and insisted on building a square one as used by government officials. Since Europeans are witchproof, anti-witch remedies were replaced on the roof by a beer bottle – at the chief's suggestion.

5 Mariyo, the third wife of the chief of Kongle, outside my hut. Mariyo was one of my best informants, a lively and good-natured woman. It speaks highly of her personal qualities that she had not been divorced although infertile. She wears the typical bunch of leaves, fore and aft. In the background are the gas burner and plastic bucket that constituted the kitchen.

6 A candidate for circumcision. The boy, dressed by his 'husband', tours his relatives, dancing for them. The outfit is very hot and uncomfortable, incorporating buffalo horns, two robes, a leopard skin, leg-rattles and a decorative head-cloth. A boy may be dressed thus for several weeks or longer until the actual cutting takes place.

7 Circumcision: the boy is stood against a tree with one foot on top of another and the penis is peeled for almost its entire length. The boy is not supposed to cry out. Here the act is mimed during another ceremony. The candidate wears the gourd penis sheath required for men during important rituals.

8 The typically squat build of a Dowayo boy (*left*) contrasts with the lean frame found in the Fulani population. The Dowayo is 'modernist' and westernized, as exemplified by his transistor radio and the fact that he is a Christian. The Fulani is a Muslim and looks towards the Arab world. He is the son of the local Muslim ruler.

9 The guide to Ninga with his pet bird.

10 A village woman sits in the court-yard outside her hut with her children. She is plaiting the bunches of leaves to be worn by her daughter. Cloth is normally only worn by the very rich or on visits to town.

11 Only women make baskets in Dowayoland (only men make woven mats and cloth). Baskets are typically made by groups of women gossiping together during the dry season. They are made suitable for carrying flour by plastering the insides with cow dung.

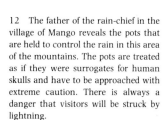

12 The father of the rain-chief in the village of Mango reveals the pots that are held to control the rain in this area of the mountains. The pots are treated as if they were surrogates for human skulls and have to be approached with extreme caution. There is always a danger that visitors will be struck by lightning.

13 Potters hand-throw pots using the coil technique and a fragment of broken pot as a sort of turntable. Potters are amongst the few female Dowayos who have access to cash. The fancy hair-style and modern clothes of this woman testify to her unusual, if 'unclean', status.

14 Potters baking. Potters are the wives of the blacksmiths. Only they may make pots and they are the principal midwives. They are held to be 'unclean' and ritually polluting. Ashes from the baking process can cause venereal disease in other Dowayos and would kill the rain-maker if he passed through the village at this time. Baking is therefore a time of some danger.

15 Carrying a dead woman back to her village. At death, a woman's body is wrapped in cloth and cattle hides provided by her husband's group. It is then transported back to the village of her birth for further wrapping, interment and skull removal. Her husband dresses in leaves and dances in front of the corpse playing a small flute. His final leave-taking consists of kicking the body.

16 Skulls covered with blood and excrement at a skull ceremony. After a corpse is buried, the skull is removed and undergoes elaborate ceremonies before the spirit of the deceased is held to be available for reincarnation. Here the skulls are pelted with a mixture of excrement and blood by clowns before being danced to the skull-house that will be their permanent home.

17 The author engaging in dental self-repair, gluing back his teeth with the aid of epoxy resin and the mission hair-dryer.

18 The author.

the loss of a unique vision of the world, the product of thousands of years of interaction and thought. Hereafter our view of the range of human possibilities is diminished. The anthropological importance of a people has nothing to do with numbers.

At dinner that evening with the chief our promised goat was indeed produced. Unfortunately, there are goats and goats. Young goats are tender and succulent. Female goats can be good though stringy eating. Old male goats are quite a different matter. Male goats are so malodorous that it is possible when going along a mountain path to tell whether a male goat has passed that way within the last ten minutes. The flesh of a male goat is imbued with a taste of old armpits. Few spices are pungent enough even to attenuate its odour. The taste comes through loud and clear.

The chief explained that he had honoured us by killing the biggest (and therefore, presumably, the oldest) goat in his herd. This, we were to understand, was an honour. The flavour left no doubt that the goat in question had been rampantly male. My own Western palate found it very unpleasant but I was determined to eat. Matthieu, for once, seemed to find it rather hard going, his prodigious appetite for meat disappearing in the face of Ninga cuisine. The chief, however, seemed to be enjoying himself immensely, wolfing down great quantities of the black, pungent flesh. We were joined by a man who was described as the chief's brother. In Africa such a term may merely indicate that two men are from the same village. What argued for some biological connection, was that he had a hump. Our waif-like guide reappeared and crouched at a lower level out of respect. To him had been assigned a lesser dish of burned intestines in oil. He sat and crunched them happily.

As a compensation for the food, the chief offered a large calabash of good, fresh milk. This was indeed a luxury. It was remarkably rich and cool, the first I had ever tasted in Africa. I complimented the chief on the quality of the milk since that of the meat was perhaps best passed over in silence. It was fortunate, indeed, that there were many Fulani near his village since – he said – they were great herdsmen. Their cattle gave good milk for drinking unlike the dwarf cattle of the Dowayos. Moreover it kept fresh since the Fulani ladies urinated in it to prevent curdling. Thereafter, I drank less than before.

The chief, unused to society, gave way to a fatigue so infectious that we were soon all yawning compulsively. We arranged, however, that the next day we should visit some cult sites together and the chief would explain to me the rudiments of Ninga culture.

Our first night with the Ninga seemed to fulfil all Matthieu's dour predictions. It was a curiously restless place. There were constant movements of cattle through the compound, sidling moodily first in one direction and then the other. It began to rain in great, wet, sticky drops. Matthieu and I huddled up one end of the hut while cattle thudded and banged against the walls outside and a steadily growing puddle of water advanced across the floor towards us. Finally, the grass mat closing off the doorway of the hut was burst in and a mêlée of frantic goats crowded in to get out of the rain. From the stench, it was clear that they were preponderantly male. The village clearly specialized in male goats. Possibly this hut was a habitual haunt of theirs and we were the interlopers. Our shouts and blows failed to move them. We were rewarded with a tossing of wicked-looking horns and a stamping of hooves. We raged at them. They glared malevolently at us. Finally, with an inspiration born of despair, I fired off my flashgun a couple of times and so stampeded them back outside. The last old buck finally fled in a parting salvo of malodorous droppings.

At this point, we abandoned all pretence of being good guests. Matthieu cannibalized the rotten lesser roof beams from one side

82

while I got a blaze going with a handful of the thatch itself. Soon we had a respectable fire going and were able to doze fitfully while leaning against the walls.

Matthieu comforted himself by reading the Bible in French. Unfortunately he had never learned to read silently and declaimed verse after verse in a lugubrious voice that did little to dispel the gloom of the place.

The next day, I was pleased to note that the chief was only slightly less raddled than ourselves. We set off on a whistlestop tour of religious sites and ceremonial artefacts more appropriate to tourism than serious anthropology. But skulls, pots and dancing were not what I was after. I paid them only passing heed. In the hunt for the missing mastectomy, it seemed especially important to avoid leading questions. I wanted unsolicited data and so Matthieu and I sat and watched and waited. At the first group of ancestral skulls, all apparently split with an axe, luck smiled on us. In common with many other pagan groups of the area, the Ninga undress to approach the sacred. As he limped along to the remains of his forefathers, the chief slipped off his long, shapeless robe. There, finally, for all the world to see, were two flat discoloured patches where male nipples should have been. I confess to a moment of great glee which Matthieu was incapable of sharing. To him, the breasts of the chief were a matter of total indifference. *He* had other things on his mind. He was worried about amputated toes.

The Ninga, in their cold, wet, mountain fastness, were much plagued by rheumatism and arthritis, especially in the extremities. The toes and fingers, it seemed, were particularly prone to cause trouble in 'old men' – anyone over forty. The drastic response of the afflicted was often simply to lop off troublesome joints with an axe or hoe. In his readings of the previous night, Matthieu had come across the passage, 'If thy hand offend thee, cut it off'. He could not understand how ignorant pagans such as the Ninga had adopted a practice clearly derived from knowledge of the Bible when they were still rooted in unmitigated heathendom. The problem seemed to become a sort of obsession with him, challenging the sharp line he had drawn between bad, old heathen ways and good, new Christian ways. He expounded the difficulty to me while the chief was muttering and whispering to the dead and sloshing beer over the skulls. We seemed like a ridiculous model of the world in microcosm. The pagan fussed over his skulls, oblivious to my obsession with male nipples while Matthieu's religion was challenged by amputated fingers and toes. It was hard not to feel a little ridiculous.

The chief's hunchbacked brother joined us and splashed some beer over the skulls. When he turned round, I was delighted to see that he too lacked nipples.

As we walked back to the huts, I tried to work the subject round to amputations via questions on circumcision, hoping to find evidence that the Ninga connected them in their minds. Had the chief given me a full description? Yes. Was there nothing he had left out? No. What about the scarification of the body?

The Dowayos, for example, often cut geometric patterns in their skin. Did the Ninga do this? No, they only cut off fingers and toes. (Matthieu looked downcast.) Did the Ninga perhaps file their teeth at circumcision? Perhaps some did. At this point, we encountered a bare-breasted woman who was introduced as the chief's sister. Her breasts too appeared to have undergone surgery. A horrible truth began to dawn. Throwing discretion to the winds, I indicated her breasts. Had she been born with breasts like this or (cunningly) had this been done to make her more beautiful? Everyone laughed. Of course she had been born like this. Who would cut their breasts? Such a thing would be painful.

It was clear that whatever else had happened to the Ninga, they were subject to genetic malformation. The club-foot and dwarfishness of the chief, the hump of the brother, the malformed nipples of all were part and parcel of the same congenital abnormality and not cultural symbolism as I had assumed. Bitter disappointment rapidly gave way, however, to a sense of the ridiculous. Matthieu and the Ninga stared at me as I sat on a rock in the incipient rain and laughed without apparent cause for several minutes.

By the time we left Ninga, after another night's fitful rest, I felt much more positive about the whole experience than I would have believed possible. Even Matthieu's concern with Ninga feet looked more reasonable.

Very early the next morning, before our departure, we were visited by another Ninga, a stranger, who asked us to accompany him. There was someone who wished to see us.

We were led across the village to a compound even more decrepit than our own. Outside, in the first tentative rays of the sun, crouched an old woman, her breasts shrunken and empty, her face greatly lined and in curious contrast to her hair – thick and cropped like an adolescent. She clung to my knees and addressed me in Dowayo. She had heard that the white men had returned and had wanted to see one again before she died.

In a wavering, reedy voice, she embarked on the story of her life. It seemed that she had been born a Dowayo. She did not know how many years ago. As a young girl she had been the mistress of a soldier, a white man. She disappeared into her hut and began digging in a battered tin trunk. Her son, who had doubtless heard all this many times before, looked profoundly bored. After a search of some duration, she reappeared with a faded photograph of a rather pudgy young man in the uniform of a sergeant of the French Army. An inscription on the back revealed that this was for 'Black Héloise' from Henri. She looked infinitely sad to hear the name again after all these years. What happened to Henri? He returned to his village but they had two sons. Alas, they both had died. Then, she was taken by a native trooper, a Ninga. She disappeared again and dug yet deeper into the trunk, returning with a certificate of good conduct in French and a metal disc that seemed to be a receipt for obligatory work on the road. She held it out to me with pride. It was from her Henri – a present. They had given it to Henri because he had been brave and he had given it to her. I wondered if her son, who could speak French and therefore possibly read, knew of Henri's rather shabby deception of all those years ago. From his pleading expression, I guessed that he did. I admired the cheap aluminium disc and passed it back to her. As we parted, she declared how good white men had always been to her and gave me to understand with her looks that were she a few years younger, I might not escape so easily.

We rendezvoused with our guide, the bird again bouncing on his cap and we went back down the mountain to what had become a sort of normality for me – the Dowayo world.

We walked along, chewing on bananas, pleased to be away from the cold and gloom of the mountain. Suddenly, there was a cracking noise. My front teeth, repaired in England after the car-crash of my previous visit to Dowayoland, snapped neatly in two, leaving me bemused and edentate.

It is one of the marks of people who have lived in the bush that they are seldom in awe of the skills of others. They are quite prepared to build houses, plan whole villages and execute minor surgical operations with a verve and self-confidence egotistical in the extreme. Given that the skills of any available dentist would be extraordinarily basic, self-treatment looked a much more viable option. As so often when in trouble, Matthieu and I headed for the mission.

The teeth being made of some sort of plastic, it was deemed sensible to effect a repair with some sort of resin glue. Fortunately, my mission friends, Jon and Jeannie, had a tube in their tool-kit. Unluckily, it took six hours to harden. A hope-inspiring footnote on the label warned that the resin hardened faster if heat was applied. A solution was quickly devised. The teeth were smeared with glue, held in place by two clothes-pegs and heated with a hair-drier. On the whole, the practice was only slightly more uncomfortable than normal dental practice though one did tend to get rather thirsty. Two attempts failed owing to the dampness of the surfaces. Again, a solution was devised. We would heat the teeth in the oven to dry them. This was a hazardous proceeding. Jon and Jeannie only possessed an ancient wood-burning stove whose temperature was virtually uncontrollable. I had a ghastly vision of the teeth melting. The cook stoked away manfully, flashing his own excellent dentition. Luck was with us. With a deft flick of the wrist, Jon whipped out the hot teeth, slapped on glue and clipped on the clothes-pegs. A blast of hot air from the hair-drier completed the treatment. The next few minutes were not pleasant. We had forgotten to allow for the fact that the heat in the teeth would percolate through to the roots. But they stayed in place and lasted till the end of the trip. The only problem was that they rapidly turned green as if in emulation of my monkey friend.

9

Light and Shade

Dinner that evening was a lively affair. Pastor Brown had espoused the cause of the water project and called a conference. His latest innovation was solar power. Quite reasonably, he had decided that it was a scandalous waste of resources to haul gas and paraffin into the heart of Africa simply to burn them. Investigation of the mail-order catalogues that he favoured had provided, after suitable delay, a huge sheet of solar panels that he installed on the roof of his house. By the simple expedient of exposing these to blinding sunlight throughout the day, he was able to entice a single bulb to glow for several hours of the night. Immediately he cut off all other forms of energy, which reduced his family to scuttling about with torches while the Great Bulb glowed in the living-room. Here we sat to eat, blinking like hedgehogs in the beam of a car's headlights. To supply the Great Bulb, large holes had been knocked in the ceiling. This was unfortunate as the roof space was inhabited to bursting with bats whose faces bore a curious sneering expression. Attracted by the Great Bulb, they swooped and circled, casting huge shadows on the walls. Blinded by the Great Bulb, they regularly thudded into obstructions or threatened to become entangled in the diners' hair. One of the endemic cats had decided to exploit the situation with some impromptu leaps and dives, bringing down bats that she retired to a corner and devoured with horrendous crunching and slurping noises. Occasionally, Pastor Brown would be driven to the point of incoherent rage by this flying vermin and fire off a couple of rounds from the air-rifle he kept by his chair, screaming in Fulani as he did so. The guests, the cat, other members of the family would fling themselves to the floor as pieces of bat and plasterboard descended into the food.

The local Catholic missionary and the doctor were also present, together with a young man from the Peace Corps. Ecumenical goodwill reigned. Everyone commented politely on the Great Bulb and studiously ignored the bats.

With the blessing of the *sous-préfet*, it was decided that the town should have, as mentioned earlier, a clean water supply. This was, indeed, an urgent necessity. Most fatalities in the area were due to water-borne diseases. There was little point in the doctor devoting time and drugs to the treatment of bilharzia and other parasites for as soon as people went near the river, which all used for washing, drinking and dumping sewage in, they were re-infected. Various possibilities were discussed. A series of wells was proposed. This would have been ruinously expensive. Wells, moreover, are easily polluted. It was finally decided that the only way was to take the water from one of the perpetual rivers in the hills inhabited by the Dowayos. This was where I came in.

Community projects such as this always seem eminently sensible. To refuse to cooperate with them seems selfish and unfeeling. Often, however, they are fraught with difficulties, both practical and moral. Motives are never quite clear.

The doctor hoped quite reasonably to eradicate at a stroke the major component of his case-load. Most of the endemic fatal diseases derived either from impure water sources or else these sources so debilitated local inhabitants that otherwise mild infections proved fatal. He had despaired of treating villagers who promptly became re-infected when they returned to their homes. Pure water was the only way to break the circle.

The man from the Peace Corps quite clearly needed a large project with a budget, thereby justifying his own existence and endearing himself to his superiors. As a source of money and employment, he would also have power.

The missionaries certainly had the material improvement of the locals at heart but were doubtless aware that by controlling the water they would be breaking the power of the rain-chief and so eroding pagan beliefs.

As an anthropologist, I was most uncomfortable of all. Although anthropology studies people, it does so at a certain remove, less as individuals than as representatives of some collective culture. Studying the way a people behaves and seeking to direct that behaviour are, in theory, two different things though no anthropologist leaves his people unchanged. While not wishing endemic diseases on anyone, I was doubtful whether the project would be pursued except at the expense of the Dowayos. Taking the water from the hills to give to the town would be seen by Dowayos as the stealing of their water to give to Fulani invaders. Normally, water from these mountains could not be drunk even by Dowayos except with the express permission of the rain-chief since it belonged to him. It was vital to the irrigation of the hills and for the support of the dwarf cattle that were the joy of the Dowayos. I knew enough of the local situation to expect that the Dowayos would be required to furnish most of the labour. They would be far from willing to give this except on their own terms. The *sous-préfet* too was a determined man who would brook no opposition in what was clearly a project for the great general good. If the Dowayos would not work willingly, they would be forced to work. I foresaw a great deal of unhappiness and trouble for what I had come to regard in an inevitably paternalistic way as 'my' people. It was true that certain nods were made in favour of safeguarding rights of access to Dowayos, but it was difficult to know how much store was to be set by these.

I never knew the end of the project, whether it came to fruition or not, whether the funding simply disappeared quietly somewhere along the way, whether it died in bitterness or torpor. The last I heard of it was from the *sous-préfet* just before I left for England. He explained that latest costings suggested that the whole stream would have to be simply put in a pipe to supply the town without any access for Dowayos along the way, as this would be too expensive. This would involve initial discomfort and adjustment but would be a more efficient use of the water and, after all, the Dowayos could always move.

Everyone in the house, except myself and the bats, seemed to have had a good time and left in the rosy glow of direct altruism in action. I was more than a little depressed as I trudged back to the village on my own. As an anthropologist, I did not want the rain-chief undermined. He was an old pirate, but I liked him. More than that, he was interesting.

The peace of the village seemed strangely disturbed. In the bush could be heard the voices of men talking. An odd humming filled the air. There was an uncanny glow in the sky as if the Great Bulb had been transported to the centre of the village by a miraculous agency.

One's first fears are always selfish. It was probably a hut on fire. I felt with strange certainty that it was mine. All my notes on local healing techniques, my camera and equipment, my documents and records were now doubtless disappearing in a pall of smoke. I broke into a trot and arrived at the cactus-hedge hot and dishevelled.

A strange sight greeted me as I peered between the spiky plants. It seemed that I was to be haunted by cinemas. In the public circle was assembled a large crowd. Just about every Dowayo capable of movement, including the halt and lame, had gathered before the shrine to the skulls of slaughtered cattle.

In front of the shrine for dead men, a collapsible screen had been erected, iridescent in the glare of a gleaming projector. Over to one side stood a fleet of shiny Land-Rovers whose doors bore the stencilled insignia of some UN agency.

Though lacking the ecological appeal of the Great Bulb, the equipment was impressive. Power was provided by one of the vehicles purring smoothly. With the curiosity natural to the young, little boys had gathered round it, poking their fingers into the speeding parts and quite ignoring the film. In a spirit of experimental exploration, they tested the effects of introducing their bows and arrows into the mechanism. A large, irate man in a peaked cap chased them away from time to time.

A group of old Dowayo ladies, dressed in the bulky leaves of widowhood, had taken their seats in the thick dust below the screen. They passed a calabash of peanuts from hand to hand, chewing gamely on the hard shells, and spat the sherds daintily to one side, devoting to the film the same half-attention that they would bestow upon their sons' goats. The real focus of their attention was the scandalous behaviour of one of the young ladies of the village. They raked her over the coals with relish.

Further loud conversation came from a group of younger women, eyes fixed on the screen, as their hands flashed with practised movements over a pile of shredded bark, transforming it into semi-spherical baskets. Later, they would plaster over the inside with cattle dung to make them suitable as food-containers.

Matthieu and Zuuldibo, oblivious to my return, were standing arguing loudly with a hirsute white man, clearly the organizer of the event, about how much money Zuuldibo would require for allowing the film to be shown in his village. I crept in quietly at the back and sat down on the convenient roots of a tree. No monkeys were present.

It seemed, from descriptions I heard later, that I had missed the first offering, a Tom and Jerry cartoon. The second feature was now in progress, a rather macabre presentation about the relationship between mosquitoes and malaria, urging villagers to kill the former and so prevent the latter.

To the anthropologist, this was a heaven-sent opportunity to conduct a little research in visual anthropology, the sort of equipment being here presented that a researcher could not normally even dream about. In previous work, I had established that many older Dowayos seemed unable to interpret photographs of human or animal faces. They had simply never learned to do so. It would be interesting to see what they made of their first cinema show. The younger men, of course, had been to the city and sampled many of the delights of modernity such as the cinema. It was certain that the old women here would never have seen anything even remotely similar. I settled back cosily and composed the list of questions I would ask. With luck, it would make a nice little article.

Travel literature is full of reactions of credulous natives to the motion picture. People are supposed to go round to the back of the screen to seek there the bodies of the cowboys who have been shot, for their delectation, at the front. Other peoples seem to have problems of a different kind. While they accept the immaterial and insubstantial nature of the images presented to them, they never believe that the cowboys are only actors and that they are not really being shot but only pretending. Other anthropologists have presented local people with cameras and made much of the fact that they point them at their feet. Dowayos were totally unimpressed by the whole thing.

Huge representations of filthy disease-bearing mosquitoes

slavered repulsively across the screen, plunging rasping probosces into human flesh. Close-ups of agonized human faces, streaming with sweat, followed immediately afterwards implying – to us – a causal connection. Martial music blared from loudspeakers on the roof of one of the Land-Rovers to accompany a map of Africa down which a sort of dark cloud spread like wine on a tablecloth. There was a vague background noise of a commentary in French quite drowned out by the man in the peaked cap who ad-libbed his own version in Fulani. The old ladies chewed on impassively, occasionally slapping at one of the huge numbers of mosquitoes attracted by the light, now busily engaged in feasting on the audience.

The hirsute white man eventually noticed me and came across. We circled each other with the wariness of sniffing dogs. He proved to be German. He appeared more than a little piqued that interest in the mosquito film was not greater, explaining with visible satisfaction that sometimes people fled screaming from the images of giant insects. On the basis of this, he had developed a sort of philosophy of size. People only saw reality when it was big. The world could be transformed merely by an act of magnification. Had not the magnifying glass changed our perception of things? The camera would do yet more. Quite gratuitously, I thought of a cartoon I had once witnessed showing a giant rabbit pushing over the skyscrapers of New York. The caption read 'If that were a gorilla, people would be worried.' I wisely kept the image to myself. Normally, he revealed, he only showed one serious film, otherwise people were liable to become confused about the message he was trying to get across. Since the mosquito film had not gone too well, he wondered about following it up with a hot little number on birth control. He had had it in his possession for some time but always hesitated to try it out on an even partly Muslim audience. Since the people here were pagans, there could surely be no problem?

It seems to be an inevitable assumption of Westerners that moral and ethical problems are the exclusive invention of the big world religions, that guilt and fear of punishment are simply pernicious notions exported by rabid missionaries.

Although Dowayos are much given to fornication from an early age, adultery playing much the same role in their out-of-work activities that television plays in our own, they are prudes. The sexes must not see each other naked even in wedlock. To do so would be to risk dire repercussions. A man would become catatonic, a woman become blind. A boy must know nothing of the sexuality of his mother or sister. They, in turn, would be horribly humiliated by reference to the sexuality of a male relative. The insistent obscenity of all-male rituals is the most common pretext advanced for the exclusion of women from all the most important activities. Really close friends of the same sex are those who can be obscene in their talk to each other, indeed must be so on risk of ruining the relationship.

Looking round the public circle, there was Marie, the chief's third wife, with her brothers on a visit from the mountains, one of them holding his little daughter on his knees. Over the other side was a venerable mother with her sons and grandsons ranged respectfully about her. It was very tempting to unleash upon them a film of explicit sexual content. It would certainly be the ultimate test of who could work out what was happening on the screen. In my mind's eye I pictured the results – everyone flying in opposite directions, hot-faced with shame, uttering cries of outrage, faces averted, eyes on the ground, genitals clutched in deep embarrassment.

There is something in everyone that wants to break windows, release mice at a gathering of maiden aunts, spike their tea with unexpected gin. The prospect of the birth-control film was deeply alluring. But I knew that the villagers would be more than just shocked in a way that they would laugh about afterwards, they would be deeply and permanently shamed. The only solution would have been to have separate showings for males and females.

Further inquiry revealed that the film was of Swedish origin and involved only white participants whose faces were obscured. It was hard to know what the Dowayos would make of that. It seemed likely, however, that they could scarcely absorb any appropriate message concerning birth control but would rather become bogged down in the incidentals of the performance. The Dowayos certainly have no interest in birth control. In this they have much in common with West Africans generally. It has been said, with a certain amount of justice, that the only material that may be sent through the internal postal service with absolutely no risk of molestation is contraceptives. Dowayos are much concerned to have as many children as possible and infertility is frequently advanced as a reason for divorce. 'Does a man dig a field to raise no crops?' as Zuuldibo tactfully put it. This is not to be regarded as foolish self-indulgence, blind to ecological concerns. The natural fertility of Dowayos is so low from endemic venereal disease, dietary imbalance and the mutilations of the circumcision ceremony, the rate of infant mortality so high, that there is no risk of a population explosion. Sadly, the German went away and packed up.

Profiting from this windfall, I was able to begin my explorations into visual anthropology the next day. First, I homed in on the group of loquacious old ladies who had witnessed the performance, all of whom were known to me by name. Accounts of what they had witnessed were understandably confused. In West Africa, it is seldom the case that there are the performers and there is the audience, the latter being expected to observe in silence the activities of the former. The line is never that sharp. The 'audience' expect to participate in the activities of the 'actors' in a way that would justify eviction from most Western performative events. What they remembered were the witty comments they had made in turn on the spectacle presented to them. Some were, moreover, so old and afflicted with cataracts that they only had a very hazy notion of what had occurred on the screen. This point became obvious when I noted that each old lady gave me a different list of her friends who had been in the group.

With the younger people, I fared much better. There were some interesting interpretations to be looked into. Tom had quite generally been identified as a leopard. Although he had no spots, he lacked the stripes that generally characterized cats in Dowayoland. Cats, in this area, are universally of the tabby kind.

Most seemed to have arrived at a surprisingly coherent interpretation of what had happened on the screen. It is true that I had not seen the film with them but remembered it well from my misspent youth. Matthieu and I busied ourselves greatly with note-taking. It was, for example, interesting that Dowayos offered up accounts of the film in forms appropriate to the Dowayo folktale, ending with the formula, 'So . . . It is finished.'

Only after several days' work did I discover that, immediately after the performance, all the men had gathered – somewhat baffled – around the fire while one of the youths – a city slicker versed in the art of cinematographic interpretation – retold the story as a folktale.

As for the moral of the mosquito film, I fear it was largely lost on the audience. Of course, people explained, they accepted the point that the huge, slavering mosquitoes they had witnessed on the screen could be dangerous and even kill a man. Luckily, those in Dowayoland were quite different, tiny by comparison. Those on the screen had been bigger than a man. Here, in Dowayoland, they were minute. How had the white man not noticed this?

Thrills of the Chase

A Dowayo village at the end of the dry season is characterized by feverish creative endeavour. Dowayos live in a world of very firm lines. In the wet season, once the rain-chief has applied the remedies to the rain-pots and made the storm clouds gather, one set of activities is permitted. In the dry season, when the rain-pots have been wiped dry or purged with fire, another range of human skills are allowed to be employed. To perform dry-season tasks in the wet season or vice versa is to disturb the cosmic order and could have devastating results for all. The hands that performed such acts would erupt in boils, women would miscarry, pots would explode. Likewise a firm line marks off male from female activities. A man must never draw water. This is women's work. A woman must not weave cloth. That is a man's task. Dowayos live quite happily within the network of such prohibitions. There is a comforting sense of place and appropriate time. The ethnographer comes to know and dread the reply, 'It is not the right time to talk of this. It is not the moment.' No amount of cajolery, no pantomime of disappointment, will melt a Dowayo's heart once it has been deemed the wrong time for certain things.

At the end of the dry season there is always a backlog of things not done or not completed. Grass must be cut for running repairs to the roof. The potter must fire all those pots hanging around the compound. The hunter must hang up his bow on the shrine to wild animals and make offerings of eggs. All this before the rain-chief declares the rainy season and such activities become forbidden. At such moments, the normal languid pace of Dowayo life is transformed. A passing visitor would carry away tales of the frenzied industry and Protestant ethic of this little mountain tribe that would puzzle those that know Dowayos better.

Dowayo restrictions on labour do not, however, end here. Within the apparent uniformity of life with the cattle and the fields lies a system of demarcations that would inspire envy in a shipyard worker. Only blacksmiths may forge. Only their women may make pots. Hunters may not keep cattle. Rain-makers and smiths must not meet. Each activity has its responsibilities and potential dangers. Precautions not taken, prohibitions ignored, all have their effects on the community.

In the midst of all this, an anthropologist comes wishing to 'study material culture'.

For once there is no shortage of things to look at. In this feverish phase of artisanal activity, the problem is rather where to begin.

It is a clear mark of the anomalous position of an outside fieldworker that he can happily ignore almost all the prohibitions that Dowayos must obey. If he does women's work it is a mere joke, a story to be rehearsed with sniggers around the camp-fire. He will inevitably show himself to be vastly inept at any attempt to actually make something with his hands. When potting he will burn himself. Carried away in the process of weaving, he is sure to trip over the threads, pulling the loom to the ground and ruining the handkerchief-sized piece of cloth it took him hours to produce. All this is part of the anthropologist's contribution to the people who put up with him. He provides light relief, a jester in shorts. A particular favourite of the Dowayos was the basket I wove under the eagle eye of the old woman across the compound. Happening upon her one day as she sat under the shady awning deftly manipulating tree-bark and reeds, I was entranced by this image of rural domesticity. There was something deeply therapeutic and calming in the elegant economy of her gestures. I would have to have a go.

The mere sight of a man making baskets is enough to reduce a whole village to hysterical laughter. My instructress wept with mirth. Zuuldibo, coming to see what all the noise was about, guffawed heartily and mimicked the expression of outraged concentration on my face. I could see he would use that later when he came to repeat the story to the men. Children gazed at me with intense wonder. There was something here that defied explanation. The form of the basket was a deep joy to them as it evolved in my stumbling fingers. Dowayo baskets are traditionally round and shallow. My own had no form for which geometry can supply a name. It was elliptical, slightly square on one side, firmly round on the other. It had a sort of lump halfway down that no amount of tugging and pulling could disperse. It had enigmatic loose ends that threatened to unravel. 'Where does this bit go?' I asked. Screams of laughter. Zuuldibo smashed his fist against his thigh and clutched his stomach. He repeated the phrase. That, too, would go into his tale. My assistant looked pained and crept away. Once more, I was letting him down.

The only sour note was from my neighbour, Alice. Alice was a shrew. The Dowayos do not have such a term. They regarded her more directly as 'a bitter vagina'. It was never revealed what had soured her life, what betrayal or disappointment had led to such an unpleasant character. Whatever it was, she displayed such a readiness to be disagreeable on all occasions that I could not understand how she had avoided allegations of witchcraft – the normal fate of tiresome or intimidating women in Africa. Her sons lived in fear of her tongue and had seized the opportunity provided by an indecently early marriage even by Dowayo standards to move in with their wives' kin – explaining that they were too young to have paid full bride-price and must therefore work for their brides' fathers. She had long since nagged to death the last in a series of ever more timorous husbands and had been swiftly ejected from his village. In her old age, she had returned to plague Zuuldibo, a nephew. Although her limbs had atrophied and she demanded considerable help in the fields, her tongue was still robust and active.

Her comments on my basket-making were not kind or even intended to be helpful. Laughter evaporated around her like dew in the sun. When favouring me with her views on anything – and Alice had very strong and well-rounded views on most things – she constantly returned to the evils of celibacy as opposed to the blessings of marriage. She constituted a powerful argument against her own case. The present occasion was too much for her. That a man should actually make a basket! Beneath her withering tongue, I sloped away and hid the product of my incipient craft. Throughout my stay Dowayos would ask to see it and collapse in helpless laughter in the face of it.

I had many reasons to be grateful to Alice. I discovered after installing myself in the village, that the chief had only allowed a stranger to live in his own compound so that I would serve as a buffer between Alice and himself. She was conveniently able to lean over the low wall that separated us at all hours of the day and talk, talk, talk. In the course of a morning, I must have received more exposure to language than one could normally hope for in a week. This was good for me. Zuuldibo sniggered and remarked that my use of the negative would benefit most. In her many and elaborate pronouncements, she never said anything nice about anyone.

In anthropology, enjoyment is often used as an approximate

yardstick of understanding. The idea is that if an anthropologist does not like anything he encounters among an alien people, this is ethnocentrism. If he disapproves of anything, this is the result of bringing to bear the wrong standards. It is often ignored that very often the culture that the ethnographer enjoys least is his own, the one that he should know best. No such strictures are brought to bear upon pleasure. An ethnographer who likes some facet of the culture he is studying is never accused of ethnocentrism or wrong standards. This curious fact has led to a bizarre slanting of ethnographic monographs, wherein the fieldworker is depicted as wallowing in unmitigated delight in the things he experiences. Possibly this is why the actual experience of fieldwork comes as such a shock to the beginner and seems to call into question his commitment to the subject.

Had the Dowayos not shared my detestation of Alice, I should have been hard put to maintain the pleasure principle that I, too, had always unthinkingly accepted. Fortunately, they did. When Alice was in full spate, railing against someone or something unfortunate enough to attract her attention, Zuuldibo could often be heard giving an ironic *sotto voce* commentary from behind the other wall of the compound. Matthieu became especially good at mimicking Alice's voice and the impersonation of her became something of a party trick with him.

Quite suddenly one day Alice died. Normally, where a death occurred with such swiftness in the absence of previous ill-health, witchcraft should have been suspected. In the present case, no one was too anxious to look further into the matter. A sort of collective sigh of relief went up. It was quite the jolliest funeral I have ever been to. Particular care was taken with the more formal parts of the ritual. Spirits of the dead are enough of a nuisance as it is. No one wanted Alice coming back. And so matters rested for some time.

I now transferred my attention to the potters, with whom I had worked before. My activities here were much less a matter for public amusement since potters and their blacksmith husbands are segregated from the rest of the village on account of the venereal disease and haemorrhoids that their activities are held to cause. It was important to work through the whole process of potting and establish the terms of the trade that only they know.

Technical processes do not just produce objects, they offer us models for thinking about other things – principally ourselves. The invention of the pump gave us new ways of thinking about the human heart. The invention of the computer has recently given us completely new ways of thinking about the brain, displacing models based upon telephone systems. For Dowayos, the process of potting provides a model for thinking about the maturation of the human being through time and the seasons of the year. The actual ritual system is quite complex but its outlines can be quite easily grasped. Humans are born with soft heads. Hot objects and animals are dangerous to them and can cause fevers. At circumcision, a boy is at his wettest as he kneels in the stream bleeding into the water. Thereafter, he is dried by the application of fire as the weather too dries up. The various processes culminate in the baking of the heads of the boys by piling them up and firing branches over their heads. Hereafter, the boys are held to have hardened heads and the heads (glans) of their penes are also held to be dry and properly male. The various changes that occur after death are similarly held to dry the head until it becomes a skull purged of flesh. The use of the potting model is quite clear in the ritual system but never put into words. It was therefore important confirmatory evidence for me that the smiths and potters, in their technical vocabulary, tie the two processes of human maturation and potting together.

As usual, research could not long continue undisturbed, pleasant as it was sitting in the potters' compound playing with clay as at nursery school.

A number of strange people appeared in rapid succession. First, there was a grizzled and bearded Spaniard who was driving from Spain to the Cape. Knowing little of the terrain through which he was to pass, except that the Sahara was full of sand and the rest full of mud with few roads, he had prepared himself against disaster by the simple expedient of coming by tractor. At a magnificent fifteen miles an hour, he had chugged manfully across the Sahara and down as far as Cameroon. As protection against the assaults of heat, wind, sand and now rain, he had rigged up an aluminium awning. Necessary supplies and equipment were packed in a trailer that he had dragged without problems for thousands of miles. Astonishingly, the whole idea had worked perfectly. He found that the tractor was the ideal vehicle for the bush. His major problem had been in crossing borders where he fell into the awkward and potentially disastrous category of one importing agricultural equipment. He was having a marvellous time and clearly regarded me as a typical English eccentric, after the fashion of all English eccentrics, in that I dwelt in the bush. In support of his allegations against the race, he told the tale of an Englishman, long resident in Barcelona, who rode a cow instead of a horse. He slowly disappeared and I never saw him again.

Scarce had his blue smoke and deafening noise diminished, when a young lady of astonishing whiteness hove into view on a bicycle. She, too, it appeared, was set on crossing Africa to revisit the scene of her birth, somewhere in the east. Most notable, was her cycling dress, with all parts of the body covered against the sun. She confirmed that she was an albino and therefore suffered terribly from sunburn. This made it impossible for her to wear the normal shorts and vest and she had a somewhat demure Edwardian air through the sheer quantity of material about her person.

'But what about the Sahara? How did you manage?'

'No problem. I normally cycle at night. I've just got a bit behind so I'm catching up by some daytime travel. It's marvellous at night. There's no one about. It's so quiet.'

'But why do you do it?'

She regarded me like a madman. 'For the views.'

And off she pedalled, leaving the locals profoundly awe-struck. It is astonishing that it is theoretically possible to walk from almost every part of the world to almost every other part yet fear keeps us from doing it.

The last visitor was the most intriguing in many ways. On a visit to the city, I had come across a rather dapper, middle-aged American with shrewd eyes and a certain evasive manner. 'You're American?'

'Well, sort of.'

'What are you doing in Cameroon?'

'Well, you could say it's a holiday.'

'What do you do for a living?'

'Oh . . . A little of this, a little of that.'

'Are you staying long?'

'It sort of depends.'

He had, however, questioned me closely on my own movements and the doings of the Dowayos. I assumed an embassy connection and left it at that. I returned to Poli.

It soon became clear that he was a dealer in African art. This became manifest when people began mentioning to me my 'brother' who had passed through in a car the other day looking for things to buy. At first, I assumed they meant Jon, my American missionary friend. So great, however, were his depredations, so persuasive and determined his methods, that this soon ceased to be likely or even possible.

Many of his purchases were decidedly dubious in that the people who sold them had no legal right to alienate the objects of which they were – strictly speaking – merely guardians. I was also a little annoyed at the use of my name. My one comfort was that the Dowayos have very little that would be of value on the art market and that his haul would not bring him much in monetary terms.

Some time later, I returned to my potters. In the course of my work with them, I had followed pots through all the stages of their preparation. The best way to do this, had been to make some myself. This had been greeted with the usual amusement by my instructors but had proved a useful source of knowledge on the names, for example, of techniques. Being confirmed jokers, the Dowayo potters had promised to fire my eccentric works along with their own more regular pieces the next time they did a bake. This would be the last time before the start of the rainy season – when firing of pots was forbidden. I was particularly keen to see how one of my efforts with incised floral motifs would turn out. They had promised to let me know when the firing would take place but I never set great store by such promises that would be more often ignored than kept.

As I bent down and crept into their compound through the low doorway, it became clear that the baking was some time in the past. New pots were stacked neatly in all corners of the compound, red for normal use, black for widows. Water-jars were being tested for leaks, several new but broken pots lay ready to be used as convenient containers. I recognized one of my own pots that had clearly exploded on firing.

The head potter emerged. The firing was over? Oh yes, a long time ago. Why had they not let me know? They had tried but I was not at home. Had any of my pots survived? Indeed, all but the broken one over there. Could I see them? She looked baffled. But my brother had come to collect them the other day in his car. He had taken them all away. He had especially liked the one with flowers on.

Dealers have done far worse things in their time. It is now standard practice in ethnography to change place names in published accounts so that dealers cannot use them as guidebooks to arrange illegal sales and thefts of objects. Flower motifs on Dowayo pots are unusual – even unique. Normally Dowayos ornament their pots with simple geometric forms. Such a pot is therefore a considerable curiosity. Potential purchasers are, however, hereby warned ...

During my brief career as a creator of unique Dowayo artefacts, I encountered a critic who, it had been hoped, was finally silent. The ritual precision with which Alice's funeral had been conducted had been intended to ensure that her departure was permanent and complete.

Life is not, however, that simple. In Dowayoland, the dead do not simply disappear from this world. The living have a continuing, though uneasy, relationship with them. Several days after the funeral, Zuuldibo appeared, hat askew, clearly raddled from a disturbed night on his bed of impacted mud. He had, he confessed, been plagued by dreams. Now some men would tell you dreams come from the spirits of the dead. As for himself, he was an honest man, he did not know such things. However, in case *I* was a believer, it was only fair to warn me that Alice had started coming back in dreams. She had had a good deal to say about the way the chief had been conducting his domestic affairs and the lack of offerings to her skull. Her principal message, however, had been for me. 'Stop playing about. Buy your pots like everyone else and take a better wife than you deserve.'

Later in the day, we trudged round to the rather dispiriting pile of women's skulls dumped behind an outlying hut. They were always overgrown and covered with leaves rather like a compost heap. We poured beer over Alice's and requested her to leave us in peace. 'Not that it did much good when she was alive,' grumped the chief.

It was an opportunity to turn the conversation to notions of reincarnation. The chief was concerned that one of his daughters had become pregnant at the same time that Alice had died. Normally, such a juxtaposition of death and new life is taken to show that the deceased has somehow managed to jump the queue and become reborn immediately without going through all the complex rites that the Dowayos use to shunt the dead into the category of ancestors. Since the child is expected to take many of its qualities from the dead forebear, he was visibly depressed at having a new version of Alice with him for the rest of his days. I suggested that Alice's appearance in a dream was good evidence that Alice had not yet come up for reincarnation. 'I hadn't thought of that.' Zuuldibo brightened visibly.

But what about circumcision? Was there any news? Zuuldibo sighed. I must be patient. Everything was fine. The ceremony would probably happen. This pulled me up short. No one had ever spoken of 'probably' before. All statements had been of an encouraging definiteness. I was plunged in gloom.

At such moments, morale needs to be lifted. Mysteriously, I received through the postal service a periodical to which I do not subscribe. It contained, on the back page, the obituary of a minor Greek folklorist lifted to prominence by the political switchback of his country. He had died, it seemed, on the prison island where the regime housed those of whom it disapproved. The researcher in question had published data on homosexual slang in modern Athens. This was clearly what had brought him to the attention of the authorities. He had been warned. Sticking firmly to his notions of academic freedom, he had continued research and come up with the even more scandalous, 'Homosexual argot amongst male prostitutes'. Condemned to incarceration for bringing Greek manhood into disrepute, he had not been cowed. Posthumously, he published a study of homosexual slang in Greek prisons.

Here, indeed, was an example of a man who turned every misfortune into a research topic. Compared to that, my own problems seemed relatively benign. Anthropological fieldwork may have its oversung heroes but it also has some heroic failures who tend to be passed over swiftly in university courses.

P. Amaury Talbot is known as a punctilious researcher into Southern Nigerian ethnography. In his own arid monographs, however, there is no hint of his real talent which was clearly that of accident-prone self-mutilation. In his journey across Nigeria and Cameroon in the company of his wife and the formidable Olive MacLeod, it is striking that as the latter two wax ever more stalwart, he declines. He begins by falling from his horse on to his head. Scarce recovered, he strikes his head against a beam. 'Unfortunately in the identical place where he had injured it when thrown from his horse in the Kamerun, and the result was delirium and several days of bed.' Once more recovered, he is fed poisoned dates and nearly perishes. Back on horseback, he crashes into a cow. He is also bitten by a snake, but then so is nearly everyone. Compared to *him*, I was doing well. Museum Studies offer us even more edifying precursors. The indefatigable heiress, Miss Alexandrine Tinné, organized an expedition in the mid-nineteenth century to the Upper Nile that led to the deaths of her mother, aunt and their servants. Undeterred, she resolved to cross the Sahara from Tripoli to Bornu, but, taking her lesson from the earlier fatalities, hired Touareg bodyguards. They shot her.

Being greatly cheered by recollections of the difference between the private and public face of anthropology, I was once more able to face the world. Matthieu and I walked down to the entrance to the village. Here all pretence at roads gave out and the mountain paths began. At the junction was the ritually important crossroad. It is not only in our own culture that crossroads are associated with all manner of beliefs. Logically they are interesting in that they have place but no extension, like a point in geometry, belonging simultaneously to several different paths. It is here that many ritually dangerous objects are disposed of in Dowayoland, a sort of convenient cultural 'nowhere' where costumes of mourning and polluting human exuviae such as hair can be dumped. To one side, had been set up several logs for the men to sit on as they made their way back from the fields. They would rest their weary bones here a while, smoke and talk. As they looked out over the country, they were drawn inevitably to more general topics and discussions of village affairs. Whereas a gathering of men inside the village would always take on the air of a law-court, gatherings outside were truly informal and 'off the record'.

As we came up, there was already a certain amount of excite-ment. The buzz of conversation was noticeably more animated than usual. It had been decided to hold the last hunt of the year! Everyone was giggling and chattering with eager anticipation. There would be antelope, said one. Antelope? There would be leopards! said another. Elephants! cried a third. Elephants with leopards on their backs! Everyone giggled.

Possibly there were elephants at one time in Dowayoland but no living Dowayo has seen them. There certainly were leopards up in the mountains, though the last recorded one was shot over thirty years ago. Occasionally, there was still the odd antelope moving down towards the river but these were really few. Wire snares, guns – efficient forms of extermination – had been seized on eagerly by Dowayos so that wildlife had been greatly reduced, most large species being simply exterminated.

In the village, there was still a 'true hunter', a man with hunting magic and a shrine for the dead animals he had killed, a ritual specialist in the arts of hunting and avoiding the dangers that it could bring. In fact, he seldom got his bow down from the shrine where it hung. Because of his calling, his hot hands – caused by the animal blood he had shed – he was unable to keep cattle. They would die.

He would direct the hunt and co-ordinate the activities of the men. The most important thing was that no man should have intercourse with a woman for three days. All agreed to this. The hunter gave them a lecture on the importance of this consideration. The chief problem, it seemed, was not intercourse itself but the fact that the woman might have committed adultery with someone else. The smell of this would be communicated to the man. Dowayos never expect too much fidelity from their women and regard adulterous liaisons as an excellent sport to engage in themselves. A man so infected would be incapable of the simplest shot. His hand would shake, his eyes cloud over. His arrow would miss its mark. Worst of all, dangerous beasts of the bush would home in on him. He would be stalked by leopards and scorpions, and risked an awful death. They would smell him from miles away. He would thus be a menace to everyone. There was a great deal of shifty eyeing of each other during this speech that only slowly gave way to the obligatory obscenities always encountered in all-male company. The prohibition was to begin this evening.

The atmosphere in the village was rather like that in a house where several people have sworn to give up smoking at the same time and laid money on their resolve. Everyone suspects the others of cheating. Short absences invite comment, longer absences interrogation. The problem is made worse in a context where men are not allowed to admit before women that they need to defecate, since this is one of the principal reasons for men quietly slipping away unnoticed.

The old men were particularly bothered about the younger, more virile members of the hunt and felt that a further strain was being placed on the always wobbly fidelity of their spouses by their own withdrawal of sexual services. Some men went as far as accompanying their wives down to the water-hole and back when they carried their pots down there to fill them with the green, fetid water of the late dry season. They did not, of course, help to carry the vessels.

Bows are not a good thing to keep around women. The hunter's bow is the most dangerous. It can cause a woman to miscarry. Hunters therefore tend to avoid main paths and skulk around the village on long detours. If they meet a woman, they immediately lay their bows down pointing away from her and will not speak to her until this has been done. The bows of ordinary, occasional hunters are less severe in their effects though no man would be so foolish as to introduce one into a compound where there is a woman with child. Women, however, are very dangerous to them, especially when menstruating. Their effluvium is held to 'spoil' the bow and make it useless. The link in Dowayo thought seems to lie in the similarity of the different types of bleeding involved in each, hunting or menstruation. They are sufficiently similar to need to be kept rigorously apart.

Men, therefore, withdrew their weapons from their huts and hid them in the bush. There, they would be strengthened with certain remedies, arrows would be sharpened and dipped in poison. There was plenty for the ethnographer to be getting on with.

The blacksmith's forge glowed hot throughout the next two days as men approached him for arrows and ever-more-refined systems of barbs to prevent a wounded animal dislodging an arrow that had penetrated it. Trailing growths of creeper disappeared from behind men's huts and were boiled down to a waxy poison for the use of the warriors.

Strangers passing through were noticeably nervous. Why were the Dowayos of Kongle rearming?

Old men made free with their reminiscences. Things had been different in the old days. Animals, they maintained, had been fiercer then. Pressed with questions, Zuuldibo had to confess that he did not actually possess a bow but in no way would this prevent him from assuming a prominent part in the hunt, as befitted his chiefly dignity. There were other things to be done, the organization of men, the making of much noise, the despatching of animals. He drew his knife and dramatically mimed throat-cutting. He was very good at the despatching of animals. Anyway, his famous dog Revenge was essential for the hunt. Already, it had been tied up for two days without food to make it keen.

The day dawned bright and cheerful. The whole village was a-tingle. In the dim light, some little boys had gathered with the tiny bows made for them by doting fathers. They practised fierce expressions and swearing on their knives until rebuked by elders. Catching a tardy scorpion they ringed it with blazing straw until it popped and burst to their screams of joy.

The men were awash with the good humour that seems always abundant in Dowayoland when men are cooperating together in something from which women are excluded. Men began to gather outside the village, coming on foot and bicycle, bows incongruously slung over plastic mackintoshes, quivers stuffed with arrows tied to cross-bars with strips of rubber cut from old inner tubes. Beer was promised.

Women made great play with their ill-temper. Those rich enough to own enamel saucepans, rather than clay pots, were able to bang them around to rare effect. The others had to content themselves with shouting at their children or kicking the dogs.

The evident displeasure of their women pleased the men immensely. It was proof of male sexual restraint and superiority. One woman came up and gave her young husband his tobacco-pouch which he had forgotten to take with him. There was a hush. Why this good nature? Where had he left the pouch? Suspicious eyes swivelled accusingly. The hunter began to speak bitterly of the whole hunt being spoiled by selfishness and men behaving like women. The young man blushed and looked at the ground. An elder intervened. He spoke gently and sadly of the hot blood of youth, of the importunities of women who would not leave a man alone. He advised the young man to withdraw from the hunt, then no one could accuse him if anything went wrong. But he was innocent! Nevertheless, a wise man would think before continuing on this road. The young man sat in silence for some time as other women – more suitably bad tempered – came and slammed down beer-pots on the ground. With tears in his eyes, he left. What will he do? Why, beat his wife of course!

Zuuldibo, having no past hunting triumphs to recount, fell back on those of his father. He was the first man in Dowayoland to have a gun, alas now foolishly sold. Great prodigies had been effected with this weapon. It had even been used on the odd Fulani. Men sighed wistfully, thinking of the old days of warfare.

The beer went round again, warm and steaming. I passed round my cigarettes. It was to be hoped, remarked one old man, that the smell of the White Man would not frighten away the game. Smell, what did they mean? I washed every day. Had they not seen? Indeed, this was part of the problem, like as not. Possibly part of the smell was soap. White men all smelled. What was it like? Dowayos have a rich series of odd sounds to describe smells, conventionalized but not strictly part of the language, rather like our 'ouch' or 'bang'. A hot debate arose as to whether I was *sok, sok, sok* (like rotten meat, Matthieu helpfully explained) or *virrr* (stale milk), to which all lustily contributed. Since many Dowayos are, to a European mind, goatily malodorous this conversation came as something of a revelation. I promised to keep downwind.

After a certain amount of further dithering, they all set off, myself trailing behind with the little boys, dogs and other camp-followers. There was a great deal of immoderate laughter and whooping. Some of the men were clearly drunk. On the whole, it seemed safer to be behind them rather than in front.

At this point, came prolonged discussion of the nature of the enterprise in which we were engaged. Some declared that we should make our way to the main water-holes, hide up the trees and just wait for the game to come down to drink. Most felt that this was far too undramatic for their current state of mind and called these dissenters cowards. They left in a huff to follow their own devices. The remaining band of about twenty continued out into the bush.

We made our way down to a depression between two mountains where the grass was long and relatively lush from accumulated water. Apparently, a man had sighted antelope here a few days ago. A private scouting foray by the village hunter had confirmed the presence of deer. The men and boys were shushed into silence and immediately developed the giggles like children stealing apples. Many of the men had been circumcised together and so had to joke with each other anyway. It was agreed that the hunter and six other men would make their way round to the other side of the valley and that we would drive the game towards them on receipt of their shouted signal. Since the sides of the valley were steep, the deer should not be able to escape that way. We would have them all.

There now came one of those dull periods of which the whole of fieldwork seems to consist on bad days. We waited for about an hour in the long grass. A steady drizzle developed, the rain not so much falling as seeping coldly into us until we were wretched. Several developed headaches and blamed Zuuldibo's beer loudly.

Finally, there came a shout from the far end. We all stood up and advanced in a line across the depression. Zuuldibo seemed to be indeed a valuable asset. He had perfected a high howl that commanded astonishment while brooking no imitation. Any living thing, one felt, would flee before that. The dogs had picked up the excitement, snarling and trying to dart ahead through our legs. Unfortunately, the dampness in the area had encouraged rank growth of thorny shrubs that seemed to have linked branches to defy us passage. It was never clear who had the idea of starting a fire but soon a long line was ablaze. It was unfortunate that the matter had not been discussed beforehand since the wind was blowing in entirely the wrong direction. We were rapidly engulfed in choking smoke and driven back by the heat of the flames. The little boys were wild-eyed with terror and began to sob. Matthieu and I hauled them up the bare stone walls and led them round to the other side of the flames. We were greeted by seven very irritated men, arrows notched to slay anything that moved. In dribs and drabs, some of the men and dogs made their way through and stood about looking disconsolate. From shouts at some distance, we learned that one small antelope had been killed in all the confusion while the rest had got away.

Suddenly, there came a crashing in the bush. All the armed men swivelled round and raised their bows. The dogs leaped forward unchecked. There was a hideous snarling and yelping, an offstage battle of giants. We advanced in the wake of the hunters. Before us boiled a tangled mass of dogs. It seemed that one dog had become wounded in the operations and the other dogs, smelling blood, had thrown themselves upon it and were tearing it to pieces in the heat of combat. No one intervened. It died a horrible death and the dogs began a lurid cannibal feast. I was the only one who seemed upset by all this, the men joking and laughing. The dog's owner was not there. The dogs crunched and ripped sickeningly.

All at once, there was a great trampling sound and a Dowayo cow appeared, looked at us with polite surprise and stepped delicately round the boil of dogs to disappear into the long grass on the other side.

One of the men, taken by surprise, had fired at it and missed. West African bows, being permanently strung unlike in other parts of the world, are not very accurate at the best of times. Their range too is limited. We were to kill nothing big that day. The dogs, following their meal, had lost interest. The men were downcast. Someone had seen a land tortoise, a sure sign that one of his relatives was to die. The others devoted themselves to smoking out bush-rats by plunging firebrands down one end of their tunnels and skewering them as they fled out the other. This was not quite fit activity for hunters, being more the sort of thing that children do. Several little boys showed themselves very adept at the more difficult parts of the operation and gave their elders instruction. As the rats were clubbed or stabbed, they urinated over their killers. Fortunately, it was not until I returned to Europe that someone told me that this is the source of the deadly disease Lassa fever. Apparently, it is caused by a virus contained in the urine of the rats to which human children are immune but which can be lethal to adults. Not knowing this at the time, I watched the operation for some time and helped carry the haul of rats back to the village.

The men maintained that they had had a splendid day. But there was no hiding from the women that they were not returning with shoulders bowed beneath the weight of antelope meat. There would be no immoderate feasting in the village that evening. No skulls would he heaped on the hunter's shrine. The women secretly knew that the men had had a rotten time and seemed more cheerful for it.

The next day an outraged elder arrived complaining that some fools had started a fire over by the mountains and all his fences had been burned down. He had been hard put to it to save his granary. Zuuldibo gravely reminded him that he had passed on an instruction from the *sous-préfet* some time ago, ordering all villagers to clear a firebreak around their huts. The man had not done so. It was his own fault. Let him return to his village before anyone found out and he had to be fined.

After this disastrous hunt there was a considerable amount of discussion about the conclusions to be drawn. I, of course, was eager to encourage talk on all these topics and acquired an unwelcome reputation as a scandalmonger. Everyone was agreed that the hunt had failed owing to the unbridled sexual self-indulgence of almost everyone else. One man confessed that he had been unable to dispense with gratification for the required period and hoped that this had nothing to do with the débâcle at the base of the mountain. Just to be on the safe side, he had accused his wife of adultery and beaten her.

The way that the fire had turned back on them, the fact that the dogs had fought each other, the way that the antelope had turned into a cow – all this argued for either adultery or witchcraft, maybe both. There was a lingering whiff of mutual suspicion in the village. Neighbours had been revealed as sexual gluttons and liars. Wives were possibly adulterous. Witches were at work.

Dowayos have their good times and their bad times like everyone else. They expect a man in this world to have a mixture of good and bad fortune and do not seek too far the ultimate causes of misfortune. They have developed a whole range of devices that account more or less loosely for the complexities of what we call luck. A man may have good fortune through buying appropriate witchcraft which he swallows or the use of charms and spells. Bad fortune may come from witchcraft of others or the intervention of hostile ancestors. All these may mix together to make the world difficult to interpret. Ancestors may aggravate the witchcraft of a living rival. They may also interfere in the operation of divining, which is normally the only way of determining what factors are at work. A man does not expect too much certainty. What is striking is the change that may occur, within a very short time, in the way that similar events are viewed. Once suspicion of witchcraft is in the air, all the necessary evidence to confirm this belief is automatically generated.

The genitals of Zuuldibo's cattle became infested with worms. His son stumbled on a rocky path and twisted his ankle. Beer that should have fermented turned sour instead. All these things are a fairly regular part of life in Dowayoland and would normally invite no special comment. In the present climate, however, they were all viewed as part of the same thing, as evidence that something more general was amiss. Zuuldibo was clearly worried. One night a little boy appeared at my door asking if I had any 'roots' that could help the chief sleep. I passed on some that I had received from the local doctor during a bout of malaria but the next day Zuuldibo was fretful and explained that he had had bad dreams.

The next night, owls were seen near the cattle. Two of the wives started ostentatiously putting up porcupine quills and other anti-witchcraft remedies on the roofs of their huts. Owls are associated with witchcraft and Dowayos have a deep fear of them 'because of their staring eyes', the same reason they give for fear of leopards. The wives were making a fairly clear statement that they knew there was witchcraft about but *they* had no part of it.

This is an area where an outsider has a clearly privileged status. All Dowayos agree that white men are ignorant of witchcraft. The secrets have been lost in their own country. They cannot be witches nor can they suffer from witchcraft themselves. On my previous trip, after a series of disasters involving a car crash, sickness and financial difficulty, I had suggested to a number of Dowayos that I might be the victim of a witchcraft attack. They had all laughed as at a great joke.

A few days later, one of the women reported that the water-hole had turned green and slimy. A diviner was sent for. He was a man famous throughout Dowayoland. He would be very expensive.

His appearance was a little disappointing. There were no charms and outrageous clothes, no stick in the form of a snake, no deliberate staring down of those he was speaking to. He was modest and quiet, dressed in a grey tunic. He reminded me for all the world of a consultant at a western hospital. He called the chief's whole family together and interrogated them on what had happened, nodding and muttering softly as he drew out their confidences. Interestingly, no one mentioned the hunt which had seemed to me the most significant event of the lot since it had structured all that was to follow. He called for a bowl of water and the women were driven out. It was set carefully before him and he blew over it several times before allowing the surface to clear. He stared intently into it for some thirty seconds. We all held our breath. He cleared his throat and everyone leaned forward to catch his words.

It seemed this was a difficult case. He would use the *zepto* oracle. Aah. He dug in his little leather bag and pulled out some sections of the rectangular cactus-like plant. Two slices were cut and the session began. It seemed wrong that this should happen in broad daylight, with sunshine streaming through the door of the hut. It seemed to call for flickering firelight and dramatic shadows transforming faces into theatrical props. Everything was totally matter-of-fact. We were watching a man in command of his subject. He inspired confidence. The motions of his hands were spare and precise. The divination consists of rubbing together two slices of the plant and asking questions the while. The plant sections stick or go in holes when the significant question has been asked. New sections of *zepto* are taken and the questioning is continued.

We began with witchcraft. Was there witchcraft? The oracle indicated that there was. What kind was it? He named the various sorts. The oracle picked one out. Was it women? The oracle revealed that it was. Finally, by ever finer questioning, it seemed that we had got down to the level of naming names. Was it the white man? No response from the oracle. The men laughed. I broke out in a sweat. The two surfaces continued to move smoothly over each other. If the *zepto* stuck at any moment I would still be implicated. It seemed an unfairly long stretch of time before he moved on like the moment in musical chairs where you have to relinquish lingering claims on one seat without any hope of reaching the next.

Dowayos know, of course, that diviners can cheat and manipulate the oracle. One expects to pay for quality, not just of the man himself but the power of his plant. To identify me as the source of the witchcraft would gravely undermine his audience's faith in his reliability.

A woman in the next compound was picked out as the culprit. Contrary to expectation, the diviner did not stop here. He took two new slices of plant. Were there spirits active? There were. Aah, this was a complicated case. The audience nodded approval. Indeed, this was a good man. All patients like to be told that their disease is special, that it stretches the skill of the healer.

From the look on Zuuldibo's face, he knew as well as I did where the divination was going to end. It was Alice again, doubtless abetting the witchcraft of this minor nuisance in the next compound.

The diviner came up with another name, a long-dead woman with no history of molestation of her kin. It was as if he lost his audience at this point. They began shaking their heads and exchanging glances. He felt it too. He began to work faster and produced some fairly fancy material on the actual demands made by the deceased. But he had lost credibility. An attempt to return to the witchcraft of the alleged miscreant in the next compound flopped badly. No one seemed convinced any more.

It came as no surprise that a couple of days later, some of the men arranged for Zuuldibo's father-in-law, also a skilled *zepto-slicer*, to run another session. Being more attuned to local conditions, he came up with the answer that it was all due to Alice and her interfering ways. Confirmation of this diagnosis came later that night. Another man dreamed that Alice appeared and explained at some length the nature of her grievance. Normally the dead just complain generally of neglect. They have received no offerings of beer or blood. No attempts have been made to organize the ceremonies that make them available for reincarnation. Alice was rather different. Just as in life she had not limited her attention to those matters that might be viewed as strictly her own business, so in death she allowed herself to range widely over the doings of her descendants. She was apparently scandalized that her nephew, Zuuldibo, was not doing more to further the projected circumcision. Her youngest son, though married, was still uncut. She wanted something done about it. I felt that at last she had become an ally.

I I

The Black–White Man

Time had dragged on in Dowayoland. My own metabolic processes seemed to have adapted to a slower pace of life. Outsiders who appeared seemed to flash across the horizon at indecent speed. I rose, ate, drank, excreted, talked. Time passed. Most of the day was spent with a local healer who had accepted me as a pupil. We went out together, discussed illnesses. (How do you know it is this illness? Is this just a sign of another illness or an illness itself?) I became skilled in the art of diagnosis. I learned how to rub slices of *zepto* together, like the healers, to divine whether the ultimate cause of disease was ancestral displeasure, witchcraft, a violated interdiction, contact with polluted people and so on. I learned herbal remedies. I learned how to bleed a woman suffering from excess of blood owing to exposure to sunlight. My tutor was as sagacious, gentle and rigorous as my tutor at Oxford had been.

Yet, valuable as all this was, I felt that I was no closer to the facts of circumcision which, after all, was what I had come to witness. We went through endless rehearsals with the impatience of a peace-time army. Matthieu and I cleaned and checked the equipment. Fungus and the ravages of termites had affected only unimportant parts of the apparatus. We practised loading film. I taught Matthieu to take photographs both with an automatic and a manual camera. He swiftly mastered both.

While we were engaged in such time-filling activities, we seemed to see a lot of the chief's youngest daughter, Irma. She developed the habit of coming and preening herself in the space before our huts. There is nothing particularly unusual in this. The compound, after all, belonged to her father. Dowayo maids are much given to self-beautification. They weave their hair into intricate patterns. They rub their skin with oil and red kaolin until they shine like antique mahogany.

After a while, however, she began to adopt what seemed to be consciously langorous poses along the logs that served as seats before her father's house. She sang odd little melodies and showed her profile to full advantage. Matthieu's embarrassment was manifest. It was obvious to all that she had set her sights on him. Of course, she was married already but this did not necessarily count for very much. Dowayos frequently divorce. The introduction of a young, unattached but highly marriageable young man such as Matthieu into the compound was bound to have a certain disruptive effect on social life. I was relieved that the impact seemed to be on Zuuldibo's daughter rather than one of his wives. Thus far, I had heard no murmur of complaint, a sign that everyone must have been on their very best behaviour where there were so many jealous ladies watching each other's every move.

Irma had not been greatly favoured by nature. From her father came her stocky frame, unrelieved by the slightest sign of a waist and the bullet-like skull that she emphasized by constant shaving of her head. Her real strength in the marriage stakes lay, however, not in her physical charms. Her great attraction lay in the proof she had given of her unusual fertility, having produced two children – one alas now dead – in the course of a mere two years of marriage. She was now pregnant again. Should she divorce at this point, the ownership of the child would make a splendid legal wrangle that the Dowayos would digest with relish. She was admittedly a little older than Matthieu but this is no great impediment in a culture where a boy may expect to inherit his father's wives or take over those of a Nestorian uncle. She would be a very good match for him if he could raise the bride-price. I knew with a resigned certainty that his hopes would centre on me as his source of finance. I would be subject to pleas, cajolery and ill-temper until I promised, in a moment of weakness, to help. Looking back over conversations of the past few days, I paranoiacally detected a common theme in Matthieu's discourse. His father's cattle were sick, the millet did not look good this year. I resolved to strike back with a few dropped remarks about my own poverty and lack of cash.

One particularly invidious technique used by Matthieu in the past, to bring pressure to bear, was to place relatives at strategic points in public places. They could then leap out upon me, embracing my knees and crying out my generosity to the world. Tears of gratitude would spring spontaneously to their eyes as they contrasted my wealth with their poverty, my open-handed beneficence with the hard-heartedness of those demanding bride-price. They would wail and shout, thanking me for things I had never agreed to do, until in the public mind, I would be guilty of the worst perfidy were I to refuse.

Over the next few days, Irma decided to up the pressure herself. We were always playing about with cameras, surely we would wish to photograph her? Would we prefer a picture with her child (we knew of course that she had already had two children?) or without? It was a pity that she had had no chance to decorate herself, she indicated her ample form with an elegant gesture, but perhaps we would be content with her everyday appearance? In a fit of gratuitous wickedness, I suggested that Matthieu should take some practice shots of Irma.

Thus it was only after a lengthy stay in our company that Irma retreated to the guest hut where she and her husband were lodged. Zuuldibo had honoured them greatly by putting them next to the beer hut, a position of great trust. Immediately, we heard raised voices, the slap of a husbandly hand and the head of Zuuldibo's son-in-law rose over the low mud wall to glare at us. That he should do this in her father's village showed that things were heading for a crisis. I decided we needed an expedition to remove us from the village until things had settled down.

It was at this point that Gaston arrived on his bicycle. There was a man in town, a black–white man, who claimed to know me and was looking for me. Gaston had sent him to the mission and ridden back to warn me in case I wanted to avoid him. This Dowayo view of the world as full of people who had to be avoided, as rich in opportunities to not see people, was one that always appealed to me.

I guessed at once who it was, my colleague Bob, the man who had accompanied me in the incident of the monkey and the cinema. The designation 'black–white man' does not indicate one of mixed race (Bob was very dark) but a black man who is westernized and behaves like a white man.

Bob and I had met purely by chance some time before. I was driving into the city for supplies when I came across a strange sight. There, standing by the roadside, was a man hitch-hiking. In itself, there is nothing very unusual about this. People in Africa hitch-hike all the time. Whole families do it together, often with most of the family possessions and livestock on their heads. The approved method, however, is to stand by the roadside waving the whole lower arm in a curiously limp-wristed, flapping motion. The lift, if offered, is not normally a gratuitous benefaction but payment is expected. This constitutes an important supplement to the salaries of lorry drivers, for example. No vehicle is ever considered unsuitable for the large-scale transport of people and chattels. Petroltankers, for example, are held to be ideal for this purpose and are regularly to be seen thundering along with rather wide-eyed passengers clinging to their rounded tops.

The present figure was unusual in that he was hitching after the western fashion, jerking an extended thumb into the air at approaching vehicles. This was unfortunate. In Africa, interpretations of this gesture may vary but all agree that it is extremely rude. Such a gesture, executed in the face of a huge African trucker, may readily lead to rage and violence. Should any female member of his family, such as his mother or sister, be in the cab of a truck so addressed, the consequences are likely to be extreme.

The hiker seemed innocent of slanderous intent. An expression of puzzled disappointment was stamped across his features. Occasionally a truck would swerve dangerously towards him, sometimes a face, distorted with anger, would appear briefly through a cab window and mouth silent words of rage at him. None stopped. I did.

My passenger, assuming I was French, conversed with me for some time in that tongue. Having ascertained that I spoke English as well, he switched to that language albeit with a strong American accent. It was still not obvious that he was not of wholly African origins. Often, the gilded youth of Africa will model its English on the heroes of the no-longer-silent screen and attain John Wayne drawls or accents rich in the lore of the plantation, without ever having visited the USA.

It was only after some miles that he grudgingly confessed to being a black American or as he put it 'an African of American origin'. It seemed that his truck had broken down some miles to the east of where I picked him up. What was he doing here? Was he perhaps with the Peace Corps? Bob's expression betrayed a certain lack of admiration for the corps and its values. He was an anthropologist. His research centred on market-traders in the cities.

He was seeking to determine what factors affected the type and price of goods in the market-place and the subtler cultural aspects of its economic operations. Since he had been so reticent about his own origins, I was silent about mine and encouraged him to give me a lecture on the nature of the anthropological endeavour. I no longer recall exactly what he said except that he seemed to reserve a special sort of scorn for anthropologists who concerned themselves with religion or ritual as I did. They were, it seemed, inherently frivolous and evil, diverting attention, as they did, from the realities of economic exploitation.

I suppose that, had Bob and I met in Europe or America, we would have fairly rapidly decided that we were not likely to get on and simply left the matter there. But so great is the sense of isolation of Westerners in Africa, that all differences seem to pale to insignificance. You end up feeling warmly about people you would not even talk to at home.

As it was, he seemed rather desperately anxious to speak English with someone and, as I dropped him in one of the less smart townships of the city, he offered the normal form of hospitality – a beer.

His house was modern but modest, of square mud bricks covered with a skim of cement. A small garden lay at the back together with a separate cooking hut. Africans are appalled at European preparedness to cook and sleep under the same roof. He had furniture, I noted with envy, including such luxury features as a bed and chairs of angle-iron. Curiously, although of immense strength, these were, as always in Cameroon, broken. The present specimens were lacking occasional legs and arms as if veterans of some withering campaign. The most wanton self-indulgence was a low coffee-table on which we set our beers. To make up for such fripperies, we drank man-to-man from the bottle. From the temperature of the beer, he had a refrigerator too.

Bob and I got to know each other quite well in the course of the next few months. Lonely Westerners tend to seek each other out in the same restricted selection of locales. It was almost two months before he ever asked me what I was doing in Cameroon, no doubt assuming that I was involved in one of the many development projects, and providing me with a sort of cameo of the anthropologist in his natural setting. When he did find out, it inevitably became a joke between us, he constantly threatening to visit me in the field.

Bob was a man of unquiet mind. Most of his problems came from being black and his attempts to adopt a sensible, sensitive and self-aware stance to his colour and its implications. He had done something called 'Black Studies' in an Eastern college for he held the view that it was vital for coloured Americans to have an alternative cultural tradition that would assign them a higher place than did the white one. He never celebrated Christmas but an obscure festival of Swahili origin. He had been mortified to discover that Africans had never heard of it. He had learned Swahili and imposed it on his wife and children for one day a week in the house. Having never been informed otherwise and having assumed that Africa was in some sense a unity, he had been genuinely astonished that no one in Cameroon could speak it or had even heard of the language.

All this, he confessed, had been in his green and naive days. Since arrival in Africa, he had settled down to learning Fulani, a language that came only with difficulty, and picked an unexciting but doubtless valuable research topic that he had worked on with a passion. In order to establish his bona fides with the local people, he insisted on living in one of the non-patrician areas of the town, in a hut without running water. It sometimes seemed that the absence of plumbing was his ultimate anthropological credential. Here he had installed his wife and three children in order to share

129

the rich and colourful life of the local people and 'find his roots'. The problem was that his wife found the local life neither rich nor colourful.

The first crisis had come after a mere few weeks. His small daughter had fallen ill. There is nothing like illness for cutting through the layers of pretension that all people use to insulate their self-respect. All Bob's African friends spoke of powerful purgative draughts and copious bleeding of the child with cupping horns. Bob wanted an American doctor, someone with sterile equipment and a reassuring white coat. In this, his wife had been in full agreement, firmly refusing the ministrations of local healers in the knowledge that they could worry about the implications of this for their avowed 'Africanness' later. Bob, however, had insisted that his child should stay with her family in the hot, noisy, dirty township, without plumbing. Bob's wife had insisted on moving to a hotel until the child recovered. Harsh words, impossible to call back, had been spoken. Life had become a strained truce.

The next eruption had come over the issue of whether or not the children should be allowed to swim in the bilharzia-infested river, as did the children of the locals. A neat compromise had been found. Bob had been forced to spend two weeks away from his research trying to convince his neighbours to forbid *their* children from going near the river. He did not succeed entirely, but made enough converts to justify his own stance. Thus he fitted in with normality by changing normality.

An unhealable breach had developed when it was discovered that Bob, in accordance with local norms of friendship, had allowed the wives of neighbours to breast-feed the smallest child when she became fractious. His wife had been horrified at the thought of unwashed breasts being popped promiscuously into the mouth of her sanitized offspring. The child was sent home to live with her grandmother in the United States, 'for health reasons'.

Matters had finally come to a head over the issue of the schooling of the children. Bob, only too aware of the potentially divisive effect of segregation in education, had been unshakable in his resolve to send the children to the local school. His wife failed to appreciate that the abysmally low scholastic levels her children encountered there were to be regarded as part of the rich and colourful local life. Since she and Bob had suffered from bad schooling in childhood and had had to make Herculean efforts to work their way through college, he could see her point of view and had offered only a half-hearted resistance. Reasonableness had led inexorably to defeat. The other children had followed the first, 'to be with their sister'. Bob's ideological bedrock had now begun to crumble. Worse was yet to follow – the defection of his wife.

Though by nature good-hearted and generous, she was slowly worn down by life in the township. The worst thing was that all the neighbours insisted on treating her and her husband as American first and black second. There was no reciprocity to effusions of soul brotherhood. Bob's determination to live in an inconvenient, cramped hut was greeted with bewilderment. One man, in his cups, had upbraided Bob in the street. What sort of a man was he to live in squalor when it was known all Americans were rich? His wife and family were ill-served by such meanness. He had even quoted proverbs at a defenceless Bob.

Bob's parents having been at one time heavily engaged in domestic service, he stoutly refused all offers from washermen, gardeners, house-repairers, drivers and the like since, in his eager-ness to throw off the shackles of an outmoded servitude, he was loth to impose on his fellows the indignity of menial tasks. This, again, was taken very ill by his neighbours, vitiating all his attempts at good relations. In Africa it is often the duty of the rich to supply employment for the poor – this was exactly how it was explained to Bob's wife. Locals refused to comprehend Bob's unwillingness to help them. The only reason could be his notorious meanness. In cultures where the pagan virtues are preached if not always practised, meanness is held to be a far worse sin than in our own culture. Where the whole fabric of social life is held together by the largely unenforceable claims of reciprocal gifts and obligations, the world is threatened by a stingy man. It was this that – added to the tedium of social life, the impossibility of finding what she considered to be food fit to eat, the general ill-will of other women who were scandalized at behaviour in her they would have accepted in a white American – drove her to leave 'to be with her children'.

So, Bob was left on his own with his project and soon fell under the wing of a matronly neighbour concerning whose relations with the 'black-white man' scandalous rumours began to circulate.

The straw that broke the camel's back was Bob's work on markets. The local Fulani merchants rigged the local market with such a tightly enforced monopoly that all newcomers and non-Fulani were excluded. They, moreover, assigned to themselves profits of such proportions that Bob was appalled. Having experienced all his life the hard school of deprivation under white domination, he found it difficult to cope with the notion that black Africans could oppress black Africans with equal fervour and complacency. Ultimately he was to break off his studies and return to America. Curiously, his dedication to Black Studies was in no way diminished. When last heard of he was setting up a major programme on African literature.

For Bob, on his cultural pilgrimage to Africa had found an experience that saved him.

For this saving of a human being, I myself claim no credit. But I think some must go to the Dowayos and – more especially – to Irma.

Bob turned up at the village some time later – Matthieu and I having abandoned all hope of getting away from Irma who had posted herself, still simpering, across the compound. He explained that he had been on his way to one of the southern cities 'for some comparative work' and had decided to look me up for a few hours. Matthieu and I took him on a guided tour. We visited the chief, the skulls of the dead, finally the men's washing-place, a haven set among trees where men bathed in the gushing cold water and lay around on the sunny ledges to relax and talk. Bob was entranced. He had never really visited an isolated village before, spending all his time in cities and those villages by the main highway which supplied produce for the city markets.

He loved the houses with their cool compounds tiled with broken pots and their smooth red walls. He loved the delicate patterns of light and shade cast upon the ground by the awnings of plaited grass. He loved the meadows rolling away to the tumbling river. He loved the mountains, jagged and brutal that rose up through the clouds. He loved the fields with their neat rows of crops.

Dowayoland conspired with him to fit into some idyll of rural peace and fulfilment. The village basked in benevolent warmth. Chickens did not screech, they cooed. Children existed solely as a source of pure and innocent laughter that trickled, like music, to our ears. Cattle lowed in hushed tones that exuded fat contentment. No youths strutted with blaring transistors to remind of a larger, harsher world. Matthieu's own radio lay silent in the red, glossy cosy he had sewn for it. Gone were the human figures toiling for hour after hour, bent double in the broiling sun. They could be glimpsed like delicate sculptures, recumbent in the field-shelters. Their elegance of gesture, the sweet mumble of their voices, suggested poetry rather than a wrangle over the ownership of cattle. The fields themselves looked suave and complete as if simply there without human effort. A sumptuous peace reigned as far as the eye could see, in some vast cosmic act of imposture.

Bob contemplated it all with love. Most of all he loved Irma. She

133

seemed to have taken to him with fierce devotion, adopting a semi-swooned position at his feet as we sat down outside my hut. Communication between them was difficult, Matthieu acting as interpreter – and interpreting with great freedom. She gave him a present of a little bundle of red peppers. He gave her some chewing-gum and a photograph of himself, suitably inscribed. I thought inevitably of Black Héloise. Would that grinning image turn up in fifty years time at the bottom of an old woman's trunk? Bob was ebullient. Irma, he revealed, was fresh and natural, the true Africa. It was cities that were bad and cities – as everyone knew – were a foreign importation. All that was bad, he saw now, came from the oppressive forces of the West. But there were still pockets of indigenous wisdom. He warmed to his theme, contrasting the harsh deprivations of his own city life with my own good fortune in living with these truly wonderful human beings. Matthieu rapidly gave up translating all this, explained to him in Bob's halting French interspersed with rhapsodic outbursts in English. 'He said the village looks rich,' he would explain to a frantic Irma or, 'He said the city is expensive.'

After several hours of this Bob and Irma had worked themselves up into a mutual fervour. Somewhat anti-climactically, he announced his departure, climbed into his air-conditioned vehicle and was gone. The treacherous Arcadian phase was shattered in a bitter quarrel between Irma and her husband. Chickens once more screeched, children quarrelled. The Dowayos could be seen toiling in the fields wresting a scant living from a hostile soil.

Bob's image of Africa, of himself, of Black America were saved by a romantic vision. Small wonder, then, that he sought sanctuary in literature rather than further anthropology. As for Irma, she was in tears at his departure but she now had someone to dream about. Possibly that was all she had ever wanted. Henceforth she totally ignored Matthieu.

12

An Extraordinary Plague
of Black, Hairy Caterpillars

Communication as a concept is much used in anthropology. From one perspective, whole cultures may be viewed as systems that govern the communication of women, goods, rights and obligations and messages. A classic work deals with the importance of gift-giving as a means of tying individuals and groups together to form the basis of society. It would seem therefore that the hopeful anthropologist would find such matters a fruitful topic for research and a useful means of creating his own bonds with the people he is studying.

One of the customs that attracts the jackdaw gaze of the ethnographer is the surrogate language used by Dowayos at circumcision. The 'talking drums' of West Africa feature commonly in ethnography and lurid adventure stories. In principle, they are generally much like the surrogate language of the Dowayo boys isolated, after the cutting, in the bush. Whereas the drums vary in tone to imitate the tone patterns of speech, Dowayos use small flutes to copy the patterns of language. Such flutes must be used to communicate with women to whom the boys are very dangerous. Similar flutes 'sing' songs at particular festivals. Such a usage could easily be adapted for more practical purposes. In the mountainous terrain of the Canary Islands, a whistled language enables men to communicate over a distance of miles that would take many hours to cross on foot. In the Dowayo mountains, however, the only people who ever found it useful were Matthieu and I when in pursuit of the elusive rain-chief. We could each visit a different peak where he was simultaneously supposed to be and report to each other across the void whether we had found him or not.

For the language learner it had many advantages, helping to clearly pick out the different tones in a tongue that – to the Western ear – made distinctions almost impossible to hear. Since the boys would be using the surrogate language extensively as a sort of insulating device against excessively direct contact, it was wise to seek further instruction in it as they would themselves.

The young man who did the washing at the mission proved to be adept at the skill and we withdrew away from the prying eyes of women into the bush so that he could point out the refinements of the tongue. Here, I was given my small flute and instruction began. It was the only experience of formal teaching that I ever had in Dowayoland. Dowayos, until the introduction of French teaching in schools, learned their languages while still small in social encounters. The notion of deliberately setting out to learn a tongue, of studying a verb in all its parts, would be unknown. Boys, however, had to be taught the uses of the flute in a fairly concentrated bout of step-by-step instruction. Orderly presentation of material, homespun teaching techniques were called into play. This was all in complete contrast to the spoken language where systematic help could not be had.

Progress was rapid. My teacher was genial and knowledgeable. He had never asked for any reward for the extra time he took in helping me. A gift was in order. The giving of gifts, in any culture, requires a certain lightness of touch. It has to be appropriate. One does not give men flowers in our own culture. Gift-giving also has to be done in the proper way. To give a Dowayo man a public gift of tobacco is to give him nothing at all as it will be immediately taken, as of right, by others.

Being fundamentally still a Westerner, I had always felt a slight social disquiet that the man who washed my shirts at the mission seemed to have none of his own. The gift of a shirt would be appropriate, I thought. There was one that had been particularly admired in Dowayoland, a gift to me, a somewhat vivid creation in purple. That would do nicely. I would pass it on.

Gift-giving, however, can humiliate the man to whom the gift is given. The pose of magnificent benefaction thrust upon me by fieldwork sat rather ill with my own self-image; moreover, if the gift were too great the man could be embarrassed.

A solution presented itself. A few weeks earlier, I had caught the sleeve on a thorn and produced a minute tear. The next time that the shirt was returned I simulated its discovery with cries of horror. The shirt was spoiled! Perhaps, I suggested, the washerman would like to have it for himself. The tear was small. It would not show.

The deception was one I had used earlier on my assistant who was similarly of eccentric wardrobe but prone to mortification. On that occasion, he had accepted the allegedly imperfect shirt and put it away as too good to wear. Thus, he had no benefit from it. Perhaps this time things would go better.

The washerman put on the shirt and seemed to glow with pride in his new acquisition. He flashed a smile of unalloyed joy that brooked no charge of ethnocentric misunderstanding. He left in a state of surprised delight. I felt the satisfaction that comes to one entirely sure that he has done a good deed. It was only when the next batch of shirts was brought back, however, that the effects of my gift became clear. Each was now slightly imperfect. Small tears had been carefully made in sleeves, collars, pockets.

Receiving gifts can similarly lead to difficulties. Not running a large establishment, I had always managed to do all necessary cooking in two saucepans. These similarly served as coffee-pot or teapot. It would anyway have laid one open to charges of deliberate eccentricity to possess a teapot in such a remote spot. This situation was perfectly satisfactory to all save Matthieu. Somewhere, probably at the mission, he had seen tea served as it would be by a butler, with tray, sugar-bowl and teapot. Since his own status – of which he was very much aware – was dependent on my own he bitterly objected to tea being served to visiting dignitaries poured from the side of an aluminium saucepan. He pined for a teapot.

One day, he appeared clutching a very battered aluminium specimen. He had acquired it from one of the schoolteachers who had been posted down to the south – a land where teapots, it seemed, were plentiful. Disdaining to take this teapot with him, the teacher had presented it to Matthieu.

Matthieu presented it to me with pride. I confess that I was deeply touched. The lid no longer fitted. It sported dents all over its surface as though used as a football. But it made Matthieu happy. I admired it and thanked him. He carried it away and scrubbed it with sand until it shone like silver.

That afternoon, we had a lengthy session with the healer, discussing different sorts of diseases. As usual, a visit to him involved climbing halfway up a mountain, much talking and smoking. By the time we returned, in the late afternoon, we were both exhausted and thirsty.

'Let us', I suggested, 'christen that new teapot.' Matthieu looked puzzled but fetched his treasure and we used it. It became clear that the spout was blocked but we rapidly gained the knack of pouring the tea out of the side with minimum spillage. Matthieu had given me a present. I had shown how much I appreciated it. This would certainly improve and cement our relations.

Strangely, all evening, Matthieu was taciturn in the extreme. By late evening, he was showing signs of distinct bad temper. Whatever it was, I hoped that it would blow over by the morning.

I was astonished to be woken very early by Matthieu banging on the door. He scowled at me horribly. 'Am I not a Christian?' he inquired. 'Am I a man of crooked words? I have been thinking about it all night. If I had wanted to kill you could I not have done it many times?' I confess to being a little slow-witted at five in the morning. I simply gaped.

Finally, I got him to sit down while I made some tea. The sight of the teapot seemed to enrage him further. He shook with fury.

Only gradually, did the enormity of my crime emerge. The fault lay in my unthinking use of the term 'christen' for 'to use for the first time'. Matthieu had clearly imagined my desiring to engage in some rite of exorcism for the teapot, so that whatever hostile spell he had caused to be placed on it would be undone. I had effectively accused him of trying to kill me.

Yet again, weeks were slipping by. My work with the healers was progressing well but this was still second best. What I really wanted was the circumcision festival in all its gory intimacy, the good red meat of ethnography.

Having no one else to bother, I decided to track down my 'wife'. After a deal of searching, we found him, squatting pettishly under a tamarind tree. A heavy shower was unleashing itself in short but intense unpleasantness. We all sheltered together under the inadequate foliage. His finery looked decidedly weathered. The horse tails, once erect and feathery, were soggy and matted. The long gowns were streaked with mud, beer, oil and perspiration. My leopard-pattern Fablon had stood up well as far as the front surface was concerned, but the sticky coating of the rear had fared less well. A thick mat compounded of hair, mosquitoes and the red soil of West Africa adhered glue-like to its surface. The bright headscarf had sagged sluttishly down over one eye. He pouted perceptibly. It was clear that this period, vaunted as a time of licence and indulgence, bright in the minds of old men, had become tedious to him. His kinsmen, it appeared, no longer welcomed him with beer and rejoicing. Rather, he had visited them so often in his festive gear that they had taken to making excuses or rushing off to their fields so as to be conveniently absent when he called. The maids who should be eyeing him with lascivious favour were all wielding hoes under the supervision of eagle-eyed mothers. Young love was a fine thing but getting the crops in took precedence. The ultimate insult had come the other night. Driven to visit ever more distant relatives of ever more tenuous kinship, he had missed the film-show of the hirsute German.

Even Matthieu was moved. We pooled our resources in an attempt to provide adequate consolation. The best we could manage was a bottle of beer and a Superman comic in French. We pressed these comforts upon him, urging that he not give way to the sin of despair. We would take it upon ourselves to find out what had happened.

It was now evident that the timetable of circumcision was gravely askew. Ideally, the cutting would already have taken place and the boys would now be in seclusion in the bush. It is ritually important that the heavy bleeding of the wounds should coincide with the first heavy showers of rain. The healing and drying of the wounds should coincide with the increasing dryness of the weather. Thus, there would be harmony between men and the world they lived in, both subject to a common rhythm. It did not seem that this pairing could now be preserved.

Since the joint scheduling of human and cosmic change required that the boys would return from their seclusion in the bush on the first day of the harvest, the rest of the rituals would have to be indecently compressed if they were all to be squeezed in and I would again be in trouble with my visa before they could be completed.

There is no one person who organizes such things in an acephalous society, no one person with the power and authority to impose his will. Matters of major public concern are allowed to drift until action is forced upon all by press of circumstance or until the moment for action is past so that nothing is ever done. It is comforting that this works so well, a proof that much of the frenzy and purpose of the world is otiose.

There was, however, one person who was indispensable to the completion of the ceremonies who would at least be fully in touch with what had and had not been done in the outlying villages – the rain-chief. It was time for another climb up the mountain where he lived.

After the visit to the nippleless Ninga, mountaineering had lost much of its appeal. Dowayo mountains are oddly uncomfortable things. They have not the bracing appeal of hill-climbing as it is known in Europe. On the other hand, to take them as seriously as the Alps would be ridiculous. You are left with the sort of object that can quite easily tumble you several hundred feet on to granite rocks below but somehow has to be approached without even proper boots. At the bottom, they are soggy and full of huge, jagged boulders that involve a deal of scrambling and sliding. In the middle they are full of disconcerting clefts of great depth but no great width. These have to be simply leapt over while hanging on in one's mind to the memory of feats of long-jump performed at school. At the top, they are bare and chill.

The rain-chief occupied what might elsewhere be viewed as a prime site, a sheltered valley at the top of one peak but in the lee of another. It was green, being blessed with year-round, pure water, cooler than the sweltering plains, well stocked with dwarf cattle (how?) and far from road access for government officials. Even the cross-country motorbikes of the police could not penetrate there, so that apart from one cursory visit by a determined French colonial officer forty years before, the rain-chief dwelt in calm, patriarchal isolation. He had seen, or more accurately been almost unaware of, the decline of the Fulani slavers in the valleys, the passage of the Germans, their replacement by the French, the change to independence. Immutable and granite-like as his mountain, he had survived the many vicissitudes of the century and still sat undisturbed under the rain-cloud that constantly hovered over his village and conveniently designated his own specialization as the man who controlled the weather.

Dowayos, being profoundly social, will seldom do anything alone that can be done together. As usual, the preparations for our trip had not gone unobserved. As we left the village, we were joined by a rather shamefaced man who was bound for the rain-chief's village for a medical consultation. Everyone knows that the rain-chief is the master of male fertility, so consulting him was probably a tacit declaration of his sterility or impotence. There was much giggling. As we walked along the narrow paths, we picked up various other people, who had decided that they would use our journey to conduct business with the rain-chief. One of his thirteen wives was there with a huge bundle on her head. Most surprising of all, there was Irma.

This was not the Irma of before. She was chastened and serious, the dross of flirtation burnt off in the fires of true passion. At her feet lay a large, polythene sack of ground millet that was to be repaid to the rain-chief by her father in settlement of some old debt. On top of this were balanced the blue plastic shoes she would only put on to make a grand entrance to the village after scaling the mountain in her bare feet. She strode manfully ahead, looking neither to right nor left. She did not even look behind for glances admiring her athletic prowess, though there was no shortage of those.

Evidence, if such were needed, of the advanced state of the rainy season was furnished by the high level of the rivers gushing down the mountain. They were no longer the friendly, refreshing trickles of the dry season that licked around your feet like puppies. They roared and gushed and tumbled boulders. I, of course, fell in.

There is no surer way of breaking the ice than for someone to fall in the water – to mix metaphors. Our previous silence was ended and the impotent man began to tell stories. One of the inevitable subjects of conversation on this path was a man who dwelt at the foot of the mountain. He and his wife were notorious for enticing in male travellers who would then be caught in compromising circumstances with the woman. Demands for compensation would be made. The husband would declare himself hugely wronged. He was very large.

Our jolliness abated somewhat when we came across the carcass of a large, horned goat rotting in the stream at a crossing point. Smashed and bloody, it had clearly tumbled from one of the paths higher up. Dowayos are much concerned with omens. It appeared that this was a particularly bad one. Their interest centred not on the fact that one who had been high was now laid low, nor in the poignant contrast between a buck in rampant sexuality and his impotence in death. It focused rather on the all-too-obvious fact that the event had occurred so long ago that the flesh was too putrid for the Dowayos to eat – even though they are inured to consuming meat that could only with polite understatement be termed 'high'.

Such incidents assail the anthropologist at all points. Could this be the bridge that would lead to some fundamental discovery about an alien culture or the basic nature of the human mind? Almost certainly not but it is impossible to predict in advance what may be important. Flashes of insight have, after all, come to anthropologists in bathrooms, while playing croquet or when dissecting octopuses. The safe response is to file it away in a notebook where it may be found years later, the ink having run from splashes of stream water, the letters smeared with brown thumbprints. The infuriating feeling is 'now that's something an anthropologist could certainly explain'. This almost always is associated with, 'I haven't a clue what that could mean.'

The death of the goat caused a good deal of foot-shuffling. It seemed in doubt that we would attempt to scale the mountain at all. It was only when Irma and I had reiterated our resolve to continue, grudgingly backed up by Matthieu, that the party agreed to start up the path. The atmosphere was tense and oppressive, rather like one of those omen scenes in Shakespeare where comets are crashing and earthquakes heaving the dead from their graves. Every time someone stubbed a toe there was a deal of exchanging of glances and nervous looking around. Down below us, vultures had settled on the goat, ripping at its flesh and watching us with tax-inspector's eyes, hostile and speculative. It suddenly occurred to me that this stream was the main source of water for the village and that we should at least move the body away from the flow. Doubts about a major water project for the good of others were one thing. This was the water *I* drank. No one seemed in the least enthusiastic to touch the cadaver so we left it in a swirl of fetid water.

Matthieu had by now stubbed his foot so many times that he was convinced that the journey would be in vain and that we should arrive to find the rain-chief out. 'Though,' he added, 'my left foot sometimes lies to me.'

His foot indeed proved sinisterly mendacious, for the chief was at home. Inevitably, the fact that Matthieu's foot had lied increased his gloom. In itself, the lying of the foot had now become an omen of doom.

The rain-chief sat, like a beatific tortoise, under the awning before his sleeping hut. This was his favourite spot. From here he could look out across the lush valley that was his exclusive preserve, watching his wives labouring in the fields, his sons herding his cattle and smoke his brass pipe while warming his chronically cold feet at the fire. From here he savoured the comforts of wealth and respect, keeping a wary eye on his huts crammed with burial-cloth payments and the young men who sidled dangerously around his thirteen nubile wives.

After suitable greetings, we were divided up. The impotent man was subjected to a whispered interrogation with much casting down of eyes on his part and many reassuring pats on the arm from the rain-chief. Irma, to her obvious disgust, was sent off to talk to the wives.

With a beckoning arm, the rain-chief called me over to his patient. Had my prowess in Dowayo herbal medicine been recognized? Was I to be invited to comment on an interesting case? Apparently not. It was a matter of change. The man had only a large banknote. The rain-chief would accept this as his fee but could give no change. I should, therefore, offer the man his change and the rain-chief would reimburse me in due course. We both knew that I should never hear any more of the change. It was simply one of the ways I paid him for his help with none of the crude blatancy of being charged.

Fair enough, but I would get my money's worth. I launched into a little speech Matthieu had helped me prepare for such occasions. It was a masterpiece of the copywriter's craft. While disclaiming all pretension to skill in using plant remedies, it placed my wide experience in working with recognized Dowayo healers at the disposal of the afflicted. The major problem in Dowayoland was in knowing whether an illness was 'just' an illness or rather a manifestation of supernatural displeasure or witchcraft. In the latter case, the treatment would be quite different. A few innocent questions from a beginner such as myself would almost always lead to a passionate discussion of fundamental Dowayo notions of causality, morality and classification. What was the trouble? The man's penis was no good. Was he sure it was not because of his brothers? He shook his head. He had used the *zepto*-rubbing oracle with three different diviners. All had said the same thing. This was 'just' an illness. What had the rain-chief prescribed? More *zepto* plant that the man would boil in water and drink.

A recent concern of anthropology has been with plant classifica-tions, seeking to determine how far other cultures deal in species and sub-species that are comparable to our own and what criteria they use to distinguish between different sorts of 'the same' plant. I had expended much effort collecting leaves and fruits of certain basic plants such as *zepto* in order that I might prompt a discussion on how to recognize one kind from another. Was it from the shape of the leaf, the formation of the fruit? As before, in the case of the rain-stones, the chief floored me with his positivism. It was not on account of any of these features that they distinguished one type from another. It was simply that one plant cured one disease, another plant cured another. One could not tell which was which in advance of a cure effected by it. He smiled cherubically. I thought of all the hours I had wasted collecting plant samples and drying them in presses so that I could haul them back to the experts of Kew Gardens.

The man set off back down the mountain, clutching the few shoots of *zepto* that had been cut for him. I sulked with Matthieu while the rain-chief insisted on preparing for us food that we did not want.

Only after several hours of tedious social niceties, was it fitting for Matthieu, the rain-chief and myself to withdraw into the bush for 'men's talk'. Even here, we conversed in the usual whispers, the old man constantly looking around like a nervous deer.

It was about circumcision. He nodded. He knew I had come far from my village to see the circumcision because I had heard that the Dowayos would do it. I had left my wives and my fields. I had suffered much and spent much money to see the festival. He nodded again. What had happened? What preparations had already been completed? Why had the boys not been cut although the heavy rains had started?

He sighed and shook his head. It was a bad, bad business. He, for his part, had done all that could be demanded of him. He had taken the omens. The appropriate medicines had been sealed inside a spherical calabash and thrown into the stream at the top of the mountain beside the stones that controlled the weather. In due course, it had been recovered intact at the base of the mountain, a sure sign that the festival should proceed. But now the whole thing was off. I gaped. It could not be done this year. It could not be done next year because that was a female year. Only in two years' time could they proceed. It was bad, bad. The boys would continue to be children, to smell bad. It was shameful to the whole country.

But what was it that had happened? In explanation, he uttered a word that was new to me. I looked questioningly at Matthieu who groped unsuccessfully for the French equivalent. With his usual positivist zeal, the rain-chief led us into the fields and just pointed. The millet plants literally boiled with fat, black caterpillars. The young leaves had been completely devoured. The drooping stems were visibly diminishing before our eyes as the beasts munched on. Apparently, all the fields this side of Kongle were similarly afflicted. There would be no harvest worthy of the name this year. If the caterpillars ate all the plants and died, there was hope that a second crop could be planted. But many had no seed left and the yield would be small. Probably the rains would not continue late enough in the next year for the crop to ripen. But what would people do? He shrugged. Some would borrow grain from kin. Others would have to sell their cattle or get into debt with the traders. All the reserves for brewing beer would be needed to just get by. The transformation of boys into men might be a wonder but wonders ran on beer not good intentions. Circumcision would be put back. The scandal of wet, smelly boys would get worse. Even the Ninga would laugh at them.

What if someone imported the millet? I did a quick calculation. It would cost thousands of pounds. It was hopeless. The rain-chief, sensitive to my disappointment, patted my arm. It would do no good anyway. No one would start the ritual now – the omens were bad. The caterpillars too had now become another omen.

Having raised funds and come so far to document a ceremony that would not, it seemed, occur, I was understandably upset, annoyed – even embarrassed. Accounts have to be kept, justification – real or imagined – has to be given. Soon there would come a point where I would have to write a report to the somewhat stern guardians of the research-funding body who had financed the investigation of the ceremony that would not take place. It was unlikely to go down well.

In anthropological research, as in other areas of academic endeavour, little credit is ever gained for negative conclusions, for false trails exposed, dead ends conclusively demonstrated, festivals not witnessed. The whole thing was decidedly awkward. Personally, I had no feeling that the trip had been unproductive. I felt I had learnt just as much during this short visit as I had in the longer previous one. Somehow, the fact of coming back had made the Dowayos, themselves, take me more seriously, as if they had a long history of disappointment through the fickleness of researchers. Whatever their own perception of the matter, they had been much more open and trusting than before.

The chief reaction throughout Dowayoland was a deep surge of embarrassment. Blushing youths were left marooned in their finery like jilted brides at the altar. Quietly divesting themselves of incriminating leopard-skins or fablon, slipping leg-bells into their pockets, those big enough stole away to the fields and resumed hoeing as if they had never put on their dancing costumes. The smaller ones reappeared, shamefaced, in classrooms to be mocked by comrades from other tribes. Wherever men met, it was a subject not to be talked about. For women, it became a new theme in the battle of the sexes, a subject to be used to scorn the uselessness of males. For men, it was a new reason to beat the women. My 'wife' made huge detours around the village to avoid meeting me. Occasions when we inadvertently bumped into each other led to downcast eyes and mumbled salutations. Since the ceremony had not been completed, we were stuck in a ghastly limbo where no one knew how to behave. Were we supposed to joke with each other, show mutual respect, return to our former unconnected state? No one knew. No one had the authority to decide for all, just as no one had been able to organize the ceremony in the first place.

A frenzy of omens swept across the country. Suddenly everything seemed topsy-turvy and every event was an omen of bad times coming. It was rather like the way, in our own culture, that a particularly nasty murder seems to focus attention on similar crimes. Suddenly the newspapers are full of them. It seems that the whole of civilization is quite abruptly coming to an end.

In Dowayoland, cattle fell down wells – an omen. One of Zuuldibo's wives was bitten on the breast by a large bush-rat when she opened her granary – an omen. On the granite paths, knots of swarming red insects were found – an omen. No Shakespearean comets plunged across the heavens but there was a small whirlwind.

In the expectant hush that settled on Dowayoland, it was time to go home. I wondered if that would seem like an omen too.

13

Ends and Beginnings

Leaving Dowayoland is as protracted an undertaking as getting there. This time, fortunately, I was a mere tourist, not a searcher after knowledge – as far as my papers were concerned. Nevertheless, a protracted bout of leave-taking was called for, a judicious distribution of largesse, an expressing of thanks. Habits of the bush had to be shed. Habits of the city resumed. As the only English-speaker for miles, I had quite naturally dropped into the habit of talking to myself. Talking to oneself or 'thinking out loud', as I determinedly called it, carries for Dowayos none of the connotations of wild-eyed lunacy that it has in our own culture. It is as normal as singing to oneself, which is something Dowayos do all the time. It is a hard habit to drop. Especially in one who had had to cut his own hair without a mirror and has green, fetid teeth, it can be initially disconcerting.

Resumption of city ways was accompanied by a most inopportune bout of malaria, something I doggedly maintained to be due to the many bites received at the German's anti-malaria film. Fortunately, I was recovered in time to make my last public appearance in Dowayoland at the ceremony to circumcise a dead man's bow.

Anthropology is a subject that many people move on to from other disciplines. It sets its bounds extremely wide. This is why nothing one has learnt is ever wasted for an anthropologist, be it never so practical a skill or never so recondite an ability. As a child, on my first day at school, I was made to listen with my classmates to one of the BBC programmes for children. At that time, it was held to be important and healthy for children to dance. Young minds were to be encouraged to express themselves in motion. Mind and body would move in perfect harmony to the rhythm of pure melodies. Our task on that particular day was to be trees. 'Wave your branches, children', we were instructed in fluting tones. 'Show how the wind rustles your leaves.' Dutifully, we waved our arms over our heads and made whooshing noises.

Little had I thought, when devoting myself to the comparative study of culture, that this would constitute a valuable experience – but so it was.

The circumcision-of-the-bow ceremony is just one of the complex rites by which a man moves from being a dead individual to being an ancestor available for reincarnation. His most intimate and therefore his most dangerous personal possessions must be disposed of. Knife, sleeping-mat and penis-sheath must be buried in the bush. His bow must be circumcised by a clown and hung behind the house where the skulls of dead men are kept. Only a man's 'brothers of circumcision', those who were cut with him, can be associated with this operation. The whole affair is conducted with the jokey good humour that characterizes all-male events. Women must shut themselves up in their huts when the special flutes for the ceremony are heard.

The ritual involves the men running around naked except for penis sheaths and ends in a little play that all men can witness. It deals with the origin of circumcision in the beating to death of an old Fulani woman. She is played by one of the men, old, decrepit, excessively cantankerous and timorous. He dresses up in the bulky leaves favoured by old ladies and makes great play with bending down in such a way as to expose his genitals. This is hugely enjoyed by all men present and evokes great hoots of laughter. The highpoint involves the ambush of the woman by men who crouch down with sticks. She waddles tremulously between them several times, dragging a long tail of leaves behind her. Finally, they leap up and chop off the tail with their sticks. All this has to happen under a special tree called 'Fulani thorn'.

Sometimes there is no suitable Fulani thorn-tree available and the tree must be played by a human actor. This part was assigned to myself. Little did the Dowayos realize that I had deep wells of previous experience as a tree on which I could draw. The waving of the arms went down very well. Views on my version of rustling were more divided. However, in the quite general good humour of the rite it was accepted as a fine innovation. Since the tree-actor is permitted only a penis-sheath as garb and has to wear certain branches of the unpleasantly thorny Fulani tree as a concession to naturalism, it is perhaps not a popular role.

All the men sat around afterwards smoking and drinking warm beer. There was some discussion as to who should spit on the widows of the dead man, so releasing them for remarriage. Matthieu and I were busy packing up. A sorcerer dropped round with a handful of aromatic leaves. I had been in contact with death, I must not forget to wash my hands with these leaves. Also I should join in the spitting on the widows, to show that I had no grudge against the man whose ceremonies we had performed. It all seemed terribly normal. Afterwards, we took off our penis-sheaths like undergraduates taking off their gowns, relaxing after the weekly tutorial. Tonight, there would be drinking, and dancing stories would be told. Matthieu and I headed for the mission as a halfway house on the road back to a separate normality. No one seemed particularly interested in our departure. There were no tears or elaborate farewells. Zuuldibo sought to raise the unresolved problem of his umbrella, some money was left to pay for the new roof of my hut. When would I return? Only God knew.

A sound rule of thumb seems to be that when the alien culture you are studying begins to look normal, it is time to go home.

It was perhaps appropriate to my present halfway position that I should end up standing in for the local schoolteacher, teaching English while he recovered from one of the vague agues that afflict everyone in the area. In the West, from time to time, one feels rotten with a fever, headache, general sense of mortality. We term it 'flu', take two aspirins, go to bed and expect to be well in a couple of days. In West Africa, the same symptoms are diagnosed as 'a little malaria'. The treatment and prognosis are much the same, and one looks no further for cause or effect.

As in various other institutions of learning, many of the pupils had assumed false identities. Rules concerning the number of times a single pupil may take the same examination are sidestepped by borrowing the identity of a younger brother or sister. Some of the putative sixteen-year olds in the class had grey hair. A disconcerting number had the same names. The problem was exacerbated by twins. Having sought the term for 'twins' in a French–English dictionary they had discovered that they were 'binoculars' and referred to themselves by this term. 'This is my sister, Naomi, *patron*. We are binoculars.'

I taught them rudiments of the English tongue from a book that dwelt lengthily on such phenomena as Ascot racing, Bonfire Night and the ever-incomprehensible Yorkshire pudding. This they internalized as 'chaud-froid pudding'. In a splendidly medieval collapsing of microcosm and macrocosm one of my pupils had declared, 'The blood makes twenty-four revolutions of the body per day.' Yet another wrote me an essay containing the surprising intelligence that, 'People get headaches standing in the sun because they produce too much oxygen.'

Matthieu conceived the notion that he too should learn English. The pedagogic urge dies hard even in one who has spent several years in university teaching. I acquired a somewhat outmoded phrase book and presented it to Matthieu who otherwise had nothing to do. Henceforth, he would screw up his face into an expression of intense concentration and greet me with, '*Bonjour, patron.* Are you of good cheer?'

After some days, the schoolmaster returned to what must have been the considerable relief of his pupils. I was free to move off and headed with sinking heart for the town of Duala.

The city had not grown fairer in the interim. Sloth triumphed over enterprise and I found myself bound for the same hotel I had used before, half in the expectation of meeting Humphrey.

The aggressive maître d'hôtel had flourished and prospered in the meanwhile. His smooth, fat face shone with self-satisfaction. With cowed relief, I noted that he did not recognize me as Humphrey's ally. He now seemed to completely dominate the hotel with his autocratic rule. The manager, a furtive Frenchman, huddled in his office as the maître d'hôtel stalked the lobby. By slow degrees, he had insinuated relatives into strategic positions in the staff. None of them spoke any language of wide circulation with the result that guests were unable to make themselves understood. Only the maître d'hôtel could give them orders. This arrangement extended to the waiters in the bar. American tourists would give long complicated orders involving recondite cocktails compounded of rare liqueurs. The waiters would bow gracefully and smile, returning after considerable delay with random assortments of orange squash, and beer, which would be set down regardless of complaint, on the table. By some rule of the house, there was always one drink for each customer. The new arrangement had not passed unnoticed. A group of bored and jaded Frenchmen had seized on it as a source of diversion and were laying bets on the relative number of orange squashes and beers in the next order.

There was no sign of Humphrey. That night I sought the Vietnamese restaurant in vain, walking the length and breadth of the town. In a bar, loud with neon, a tourist sat across from a man whom I recognized, despite his mirrored sunglasses, as Precocious. The tourist was raucously relating an adventure from his hotel. 'So there was this knocking on the door at one in the morning. Gave me a start. Then this voice shouted, "Hey, have you got a woman in there?" I shouted back that I hadn't. There was this crash. The door flew open and someone threw a woman in.' He rocked with laughter. Precocious looked impassive. He could see no cause for humour. The man tried to explain. 'No, you see. When they asked if I had a woman in there, I thought ...' Precocious brightened. 'Womans? You want womans?'

'No, I was just explaining this story ...'

'I take you to fine womans.'

I left them to it and traipsed back to the hotel.

The journey to the airport the next day took hours. The president was making some sort of a public visit to the town which meant that whole areas had been sealed off. Many roads were closed. I huddled uncomfortably in the back of the taxi, carrying a large Dowayo water-pot on my knees like a yokel, waiting for the inevitable attempt to introduce further passengers. The driver took exotic detours to avoid barriers. Some seemed to involve driving through people's gardens. We came to a halt at an intersection. A policeman stopped us sternly. 'Stop. Here comes *Monsieur le président.*' An expectant hush settled over the crowd. Soldiers and police unbuttoned their holsters. I leaned out of the window. For a second, there was no movement. Then, with infinite slowness, a baffled old man rounded the corner on a rusty bicycle. Intimidated by the attention of so many people, by so many gaping mouths, he bent low over the handlebars and pedalled furiously. Several large policemen leapt on him and dragged him away to the cheers of the crowd. The sergeant in front noticed my grin. 'Stop laughing!' he screamed. 'You are mocking the president.' The driver gave a nervous glance at me and shot off at speed. It appeared that this was a reflex he had developed in the course of many years' dealings with the law. He unloaded me without further incident at the airport, cheerfully pocketing my grateful tip. Furtively clutching my pot, I lurked in a dark corner until the reservations desk opened, hoping that I looked inconspicuous. This, however, was Duala. I stood about as much chance as a non-swimmer in a pool of sharks. A small sharp-looking man homed in on me, looking me over appraisingly, watchful eyes noting – no doubt – the sweat on the forehead, the tight clasping of the pot. 'Paris flight?' he asked. I nodded. He executed one of those sharp intakes of breath beloved of garage mechanics as they survey the damage. It appeared that the flight was very heavily booked. Indeed all the seats had been sold several times. Fortunately, however, he had a friend who worked at the desk. For 10,000 francs he could get me a seat on that plane ... Outraged, I sent him packing. Did he not know I had been here before? I was wise to such tricks. He shrugged and moved away. Later I saw a worried German passing him notes.

As more and more people arrived, as more and more furtively passed over money, confidence began to wane. I totted up how much it would cost to spend another night in Duala. Perhaps at this very moment I was being sought by the entire Duala police force for mocking the president. I would be easy to find. A white man with green teeth and a pot. Perhaps I should abandon the pot and keep my mouth closed. Paranoia set in. After another half hour, I was ready to do a deal. I sought out the tout. We haggled bitterly. I declared that I only had 2,000 francs. I offered him the pot. Finally we agreed and he sidled over to the man at the desk.

There was a deal of whispering and shaking of heads. Hands passed briefly under the counter. My ticket was stamped. I was on! I looked at all the others queuing before the desk, innocently unaware that they would never see the inside of the plane. I felt sorry for them, as I lugged my pot past the immigration desk.

The plane was, quite simply, empty. The others at the desk were embarked on a charter flight. The six or seven of us who shared the plane until its first stop were almost lost inside. There was even a spare seat for the pot that haunted me, albatross-like. It came as some comfort to learn that I was not the only one who had been bilked, two of my fellow passengers admitting to at least the same amount of credulity as myself.

The only comfort was to be derived from one even more gullible. He had purchased what was clearly a Precocious-type pendant in a bar, being assured that it was '8,000 years old'. The canny salesman had warned the traveller that this piece was so rare, so valuable, of such cultural importance to the Cameroonian nation, that it could not be legally exported. However, fortunately, this man had a friend in the customs service at the airport. For a further sum, it could be arranged that the man would be able to get it on the plane ...

The air-conditioned tedium of the flight seemed like a good time to draft a report to the research council. I dug down in my bag for the appropriate form and found it nestling under the health insurance policy that forbade me to go hang-gliding or to use power-assisted woodworking tools whilst among the Dowayos.

Writing a report is a dangerous thing. Once written it *becomes* the fieldwork and takes on a life of its own. It becomes impossible to think of what one has done in any other way. The experience is packaged and sealed. Possibly, I should simply not mention the non-occurrence of circumcision. It was hard to believe that anyone would notice. I could simply dwell on things I *had* done. A neat summation of the work with Dowayo healers would imply that this is what I had deliberately set out to do. Research bodies normally assume that the world moves in straight lines according to the programme laid down by the researcher. The ethnographer is omniscient and smoothly competent, a well-oiled investigative machine. All anthropologists, however, know that research proposals are works of fiction. They almost all boil down to one simple request. 'I think such and such might be interesting. Can I have some money to go and look?'

The fact that so many return to rather uncomfortable and sometimes dangerous parts of the world is eloquent testimony to both the shortness of the human memory and the weakness of common sense in the face of sheer curiosity.

I put away the form and waited for inspiration to strike.

A trip terminated always brings a sense of sadness at the passing of time, the rupturing of relationships. Combined with this is a very basic sense of relief at returning, relatively unscathed, to a world that is secure and predictable, where plagues of black, hairy caterpillars do not overturn the cosmic timetable. It leads too to fresh ways of seeing ourselves – which is perhaps why anthropology is ultimately a selfish discipline.

Old colonial ties mean that most Cameroonian flights pass via Paris. I stopped off for a few hours to change planes, depositing my water-jar gratefully in a left-luggage locker.

As a contrast to the steamy delights of Duala, I took a seat in an extremely chic pavement café by the Paris Opéra, passing the time by watching the passers-by. An extremely ragged tramp appeared and sized up the clientele, much as the airport tout had appraised travellers. Indeed, the resemblance was made closer by the fact that this man was also black. He turned to the seated crowd and tapped his nose in the conventional French gesture of conspiratorial knowledge and drew from inside his coat a large, plastic rat.

Whenever any young lady of particularly glacial elegance passed by, and in that location they were legion, he would propel the rat by its tail so that it appeared alive and seemed indeed to leap upon the bosom of the victim. The results were most gratifying. Some screamed, some fled, some beat him about the head with their handbags.

After a dozen or so assaults, he passed round the tables with his hat and collected a fair sum of money. The label showed it to have been made in Cameroon. To a Dowayo all this would be a powerful omen of something. It served at least as a recall to duty. I drew out the report form I had to send to the research council and, taking a deep breath began, 'Owing to an extraordinary plague of black, hairy caterpillars . . .'